Lies Swings and Roundabouts

By Emma Hydes

Lies, Swings and Roundabouts

With thanks to all my friends and
family for their constant love
and support.

This edition published in 2008

by Emma Hydes

Copyright © Emma Hydes 2008

Emma Hydes asserts the morel right to
be identified as the author of this work

ISBN 978-0-9558549-0-3

*This book is a work of fiction.
Names, characters, places and incidents
are used fictitiously.
Any resemblances to the names or characteristics
of actual persons or events, or locals
is entirely coincidental and unintended*

This book is dedicated to Frances

Chapter one

A pathological liar is someone who often embellishes his or her stories in a way that he or she believes will impress people. It may be that a pathological liar is different from a normal liar in that a pathological liar believes the lie he or she is telling to be true. He or she sometimes is seen to have a serious mental problem that needs to be rectified. Psychiatrists may agree that pathological lying is often the result of mental disorder or low self esteem.

Sample taken from an online encyclopedia.

My name is Mia Preston. I was born on first of June nineteen eighty six, the same day as Marielyn Monroe. I was born in the downstairs bathroom in the Shelton hotel in London. My mother was nineteen year old Jennifer Preston former student of University of London, performing arts, and an upcoming star.

Jennifer was literally, a drama queen. I wasn't born in the bathroom because she had no where else to go. I was born there because that was where the journalists were having an interview with a current celebrity. My mother wanted to steal their reporters.

So there I was, crowning and appearing for my newspaper debut on the cold tile floor surrounded by 'The Daily Mail', 'The Sun' and 'The Daily Mirror' and Jennifer got the publicity she needed. You are welcome!

Well that was it. We were off! We went to some fantastic places like New York, Santa Cruz, Pretoria and to some places I can't even say. My vocabulary is a mixture of many different words, full of various accents and languages. I never went to school, I always had a private tutor. Jennifer would hire someone to be there before we arrived in the country and they would teach me Maths, Science and Languages. The tutors would talk in their native tongue, so I would learn in that language. Sometimes the only people who talked English were Jennifer and the people who worked for her.

I think I'm very lucky, the exposure I had to all these different cultures other kids can only dream about. I know the alphabet and my times-tables in ten different languages.

Whenever I was mentioned in the newspapers I was known as the bathroom baby! Thanks to Jennifer always being in the lime-light I don't think people even knew my name. I followed her around everywhere and by the age of six I was doing her make up and her hair. Her little Style Guru. Although I could not stand her arrogance or her conceitedness we were a pretty good team.

Nineteen years later and we were back in London to stay. It was the first time I had ever had a permanent address. It looked, felt and smelt like home, I loved it. Like nowhere else on earth. You can travel all around the world but as Judy Garland rightly said in Wizard of Oz, *"There is no place like home"*.

I was drinking a latte in Starbucks, and the book I was reading lay open on the table in front of me. I had read three chapters nonstop and my eyes where getting tired. It was the middle of November yet it only felt like yesterday I was sunbathing on the beaches in California. I looked out the window and watched the individual flakes of snow, fall from the heavens and land on the window ledge next to me. Snow is like a magical blanket. It covers up the grey, cold, ugly streets and makes everything beautiful. I was pulled away from my thoughts when the door opened. I retracted my feet and curled up my toes trying to protect them from the icy wind. The snow came pouring in to the café and along with it strolled a tall gentlemen, about 6 feet 2, Wearing a long black coat and smart black shoes. Well at least I think they were smart, you could just see the gleam under the snow that had piled high on top of them. His hair was slicked back and his nose and cheeks were glowing pink from the cold air outside. A lawyer! I thought to myself. I little game I play sometimes. A lawyer was lucky, he could have been on the run, but he looked too comfortable. He could have worked for the MI5, working under cover, but there was another man across the room on his mobile phone who worked for them. He and a lady friend were talking about their next mission, or so I imagined. The tall man looked around the room as if looking for someone. He then walked over to the counter. He took out a platinum credit card and paid for his mocha-chino and looked around to find a place to sit. You know how you turn your head to find something, anything interesting to look at so as not to draw attention to yourself, even though you know that you are inconspicuous anyway. Well I did that, praying in my head that he wouldn't sit next to me. Even though I felt so terribly lonely and was screaming for some company.

He didn't sit next to me. He sat at the next table with his back against the window and got out his newspaper. I leaned in slightly to see what page he was reading, it just so happened to be about Jennifer and her battle at the airport where she was 'molested' by fans on the way back from Ottawa and how now she was back in England for what seemed like for good. She wasn't really molested, it was just a load of her fans wanting autographs. She thinks if she ignores them and acts like she just wants to get home it will leave them thirsting for more. Which it surprisingly does. People just can't get enough of her. There was a big picture of her at the airport with her sunglasses on, I had my arm around her and you could just see the side of my head poking out behind hers.

I looked up at the tall mans face, he was beautiful. Brown eyes, a small button nose and shapely lips, he had a cleft chin and a chiseled jaw. He looked quite young, early twenties maybe? As he read the article his facial expression didn't change. He didn't seem to be too interested in what he was reading and he quickly turned to the sports section.

I sat there for a little while longer hoping that this sinking feeling would go. Jennifer had an audition tonight for a West End production of 'Orpheus in the Underworld' and I always manage to take on her stress.

He lit a cigarette and blew out puffs of blue cloud up into the air conditioning. God I'd kill for one of those. I don't even smoke but it looked so inviting, and he looked so sexy holding it. If only I was that cigarette being placed gently on those lips. Lucky thing. Ooo, now, now!

I fidgeted in my seat and decided I had been there long enough. Three hours to be exact, they would have to start charging me rent if I stayed any longer. I stood up to leave and clumsily knocked over my now cold, unfinished latte with my elbow. I reached for my book *Escape*, that I was half way through reading to try and save it but I was too slow. All over the open page of chapter seven 'Girl' and what was worse, I slightly splashed Him.

"Argh!" He yelped jumping up out of his seat.

"I am *so* sorry! I am so clumsy, are you really wet?"

"No." He said coldly. "Don't worry the coat only costs £80 to dry clean!"

"I am really, very sorry. Please send me the bill." What was I saying? I wouldn't pay that much to have a sleeve washed!

He looked up at me with a scowl and then brushed his coat off with a napkin. "No, no need, it should be alright, did it have sugar?"

I looked at his face, and even though it had three sugars, I shook my head.

"Good."

I smiled as politely as I could and picked up my ruined book. He took it from me and looked at it in dismay, as if he were holding a spoiled million pound cheque.

"Your book is ruined!" He said examining it. The pages where stuck together and wrinkled. "Escape?" He read the title. "Not meaning to be sexist but that's a bit of a mans book isn't it?"

"I know, I like reading about men's perception on love, I find it a lot more romantic than a women's." Why was I telling him this?

He flicked the sticky pages to the inside front cover where I had scribbled down my name and my new address. He handed it back to me and wiped his hand on a napkin "It's a good one." He smiled, sat back in his seat and picked up his newspaper. Conversation over, and I think I'd been forgiven. I picked up my coffee cup and the soggy paper towels that I had used to clean up my mess and put them in the nearest bin along with my ruined book.

Outside was hellishly cold. Hell and cold don't usually go together in the same sentence, but today I felt it was quite fitting. It was still snowing and people were bustling by, clutching at their collars to keep 'Jack Frost' from biting at their jugulars. I did the same and started walking towards home. The sky was grey and you could see a little white ring of light where the sun was trying to shine through the clouds. I could hear children playing in the park, building snowmen and making snow angels. The traffic was moving along very slowly. Every now and then there was a wheel spin and a honk of a horn.

The tall buildings loomed above my head and made, what was already a dull day even worse. The streetlights flickered on and people started closing their little shops to go home. I walked slowly, listening to the sound of the snow crunching under my boots and the come and go of strangers' conversations. I loved the lives they lived in those moments, good or bad. But just the fact that they had someone special to share those intimate details of their lives with, they all had something I didn't, companionship.

I turned the rusty key, to our apartment in, the lock and stepped in to the hospital like hallway. One light was flickering on and then off and as I turned on the others the heating started to crank up. Considering Jennifer was a famous actress you would have thought she could have found us a better place. But then I remembered, she had left that up to me without my knowledge, until the last minute, Typical.

I stepped into the cold corridor and gently shut the door behind me. Leaving the settling snow outside and bracing the biting air inside.

"Jennifer?" My voice bounced off the walls along with the chatter of my teeth.

"In here honey."

"Please take off you're boots, Marie doesn't want snow draped through the hall."

Marie was Jennifer's maid and had the most terrible Italian accent. Usually I find the Italians most endearing but she was without a doubt the foulest person I have ever met. She completely ignores my existence most of the time. She will gladly cook for Jennifer, but I won't get as much as a lump of cheese, if she had anything to do with it. She had traveled round with us for years. Jennifer says she's allowed to go back to Italy now we're back in England but Marie insists, *'No, you need'a someone to look after you,'* and always looks at me coldly. I want to shout. It's not my job to look after her, I'm the child! I know this sounds incredibly mean, and yes she's only doing her job, she is *Jennifer's* maid after all, but that should not stop her being nice to me. I'm sure she thinks I'm a waste of space.

I reluctantly took off my big coat, gloves and boots. It was just as cold in here as it was outside.

I walked down the corridor with the lights flickering above my head and into the bathroom.

The bathroom was lit up with candles, it would have looked quite romantic, but Jennifer insists on having so many that it is just as bright as having the main light on. I keep telling her that burning so many is a complete fire hazard and it's against apartment regulations but she never listens. Especially if it means she cannot do something that she wants to do. That is probably why she is so successful. Her first audition she ever had, the people judging told her that she could not dance and she had no rhythm. So she paid for dance lessons. Two weeks later she had already past grade three dance and tap and got the lead role.

I liked the bathroom, it was the nicest room in the apartment and probably in the whole building. The mouldings that ran around the walls were of beautiful angels playing trumpets. The room had a theme of white, green and gold. The bath stood in the middle of the room with a polar bears skin lying underneath. The bath was white with golden taps and gold lion's feet. The suede full-length green curtains were drawn, Jennifer had sounds of the ocean playing and the room felt cozy. To Jennifer this was the most important room in the house so it had to be perfectly decorated. The bath alone had cost her £2000. She says the bathroom is the place where you step into in the morning an ugly caterpillar and come out a beautiful butterfly.

Jennifer sat with her back to me looking at her reflection in the mirror. This was a daily ritual, one not to be questioned. The bathroom was a lot warmer and I could feel my shoulders slowly relax.

"Do I look old?" She asked softly. I looked her up and down, at her long raven black hair falling down her slender back and resting on the curve of her spine. She was an English size eight, which is quite good going for a thirty eight year old. She was wearing a soft green silk nightgown that did up like a corset at the back. The colour, she says, helps bring out her eyes, even though it was just a nightgown. Her skin was so soft and clear it was almost transparent.

"Jennifer, you look lovely."

"Yes but do I look old?" She asked me earnestly

She knew that she did not look a day over thirty. Some people, think *I'm* older, which is very disheartening!

"You know you don't look a day over thirty!"

"But is that good enough these days?" She looked down at the newly placed engagement ring on her finger and twisted it with her other hands thumb and index finger.

"Has Jim said something?" Jim was the new beau. She has been worrying more about life's little tribulations with him so I guess she was feeling pretty serious about this one.

"No he hasn't, he wouldn't, even if he wanted to, he's too kind. No it's just he's younger than me. I'm worried I'll get older and he won't want to look at me anymore, let alone touch me, or..." Her voice trailed off and she looked back up at the mirror again. Jim was lovely to her, he was nearer my age than hers but he suited her and she suited him.

I ran my fingers through her clean, tangle free hair and kissed the top of her head. "Jennifer, he's dated his share of younger *girls*." I stressed *girls*. " And now he's ready to be with a real *woman*. As you grow old, so will he. You'll grow together and that's how a relationship should be."

Like I'd know, I've never had a relationship in my life. A Spanish boy turned me down when I was 10 and I have never been interested in *boys* since. Maybe I should start looking for a man myself, not a boy. I was at that awkward age where I was in the middle, boys where still attractive but older men were too and it was hard to work out which best suited me. My mind wondered back to the tall man in the café.

"Anyway." began Jennifer "My make up and hair, I have to look wonderful tonight. They all know who I am and my capabilities, I'm proving to them that what they have heard is true and they will have no choice but to give me the part!"

I think she was convincing herself more than anything there. I reached out for the vanity case, and swiveled her chair around to face me.

"What are we going for, intellectual or romantic?" I asked. "Innocent" She winked and shut her eyes. I tilted her chin up towards me, and swooped green and silver dust over her thin eyelids.

"There we are." I said turning her to face the mirror so she could see my handy work.

"Oh, lovely, I like the hair!" She patted it up, then put on her long silver, snake chain earrings.

"I'll go and get dressed. What are you going to wear?"

"I thought I'd just wear this." I said parting my arms and looking down at myself. I realized then what I was wearing. Dark-green jeans. They used to be black but they were so worn with age. A long stretched beige jumper and my hair looked like I had been dragged through a hedge backwards. What must that tall man have thought of me?

Jennifer stopped and looked at me in dismay. Before she could say anything I quickly added. "Maybe not, I'll wear my black dress."

"As long as you don't look prettier than me." She smiled and walked away. Her stiletto-heeled slippers clip-aty-clopped as she walked down the corridor.

I sat down in her chair and looked at myself in the mirror.

She says she's worried but I think I've got more worry wrinkles than she and I'm only nineteen. I looked nothing like Jennifer, where she has green eyes I have brown and my hair is a honey blonde, not black. I have freckles on my nose that I've hated for as long as I can remember and when I catch the sun in the summer they become really prominent. Jennifer says that most girls would kill for freckles. I don't believe her. I'd like it if she said she'd kill for freckles, but that would be admitting that I had something she didn't and she would never be heard to admit that. We have the same slender figure but she's slightly smaller in height. Jennifer and I have the same mouth though, a prominent 'M' shape in the middle of the top lip and as she says, a nice juicy bottom lip. I'm not ugly, I think I'm actually quite pretty, just a different pretty than Jennifer. She's a 'Rare beauty' according to the critics and I'm just plain old Mia who blends into the background and never causes a fuss.

I wasn't jealous of her success, I had played a big part in it from the start, and I'm glad it happened the way it did, otherwise I think Jennifer would have put me up for adoption. (But people loved her even more because she didn't.) Apparently she was an inspiration to other young girls at the time, in the same situation.

No, I was jealous of the time stardom took up. She never played with me when I was little. That was always the job of the current boyfriend or my tutor. She was always too busy to stop and look at me and say, "Wow Mia, you look beautiful today" or "what would you like to do for your birthday?" Or give me a kiss good night and say "I love you." Words I only ever heard in movies.

Jennifer's eternity ring, which my father had given her, lay on the dresser. I picked it up, it's green emerald shone as I placed it loving on my ring finger. The only constant thing my mother wore. Even though, now she has been engaged three times she refuses not to wear it. I loved her that. She kept my father in her heart, always.

I reached for Jennifer's exquisite Vanity case and applied some of her £50 foundation and £80 peach-gold lipstick. I then quickly reached for a tissue to rub it off. Jennifer has more of an orange complexion and her make up doesn't suit my pale skin. I rummaged through and found an old pink lipstick and eye shadow. I usually only wore a bit of foundation and eyeliner, not really much make up at all. I dusted my eyes and applied the lip stick. Then I was reminded why I didn't wear much make up.

"Oh darling you're not going out looking that are you? You look like a hooker."

I forced a smiled at Jennifer as she dramatically re-entered the bathroom. She was wearing a soft green gown, it looked a lot like the nightgown she had on a few minutes ago.

She turned around to reveal her smooth back and tiny waist, "Could you zip me up darling, I don't bend that way."

I did as I was told and let her sit back down in her chair.

"Could you go through some of my lines that I'm using for my audition?"

Before I could answer she thrust a copy of the score at me. "Right, act one, scene three."

Chapter two

"Do you enjoy writing Hilary?" I looked up at the man who spoke, in his Giorgio Armani suit and perfectly styled hair. Not taking his eyes off me as he walked away, sat down behind his desk and retrieved his notes. The copper plaque on his desk, read Doctor Grey. Everything in the room was brown or green, the desk, the walls and the floor were brown. The chair covers and curtains were a royal green. It was like being in a big tree. I looked out of the window and my eyes fell on the beautiful Maple tree that stood tall and lush in the midday sun. The wind gently blew the leaves and they danced elegantly upon the breeze. I wished I were out there, not in this clammy office with its poor excuse for air conditioning. I thrived when I was outside in the warm summer air. I loved to lay in the cool grass and watch the birds fly overhead. I liked to pretend that they would swoop down and carry all my burdens away on their backs so just for a few moments I could be still.

"Hilary, what are you writing about?"
I was writing a journal. Not a *dear diary, today I did,* journal. but more like an autobiography, a story about my life. But I wasn't going to tell him that because he would want to read it and analyze it and I did not want my life analyzed.

"It's a story."

"Lovely." Said the Doctor and wrote something in his notebook. "What's it about?"

"What's your name?" I asked dodging his question.

"You know my name Hillary, well you should, I tell you everyday." He said studying my face.

"Why do you tell me everyday?"

"Because you ask me everyday." He did another scribble in his book. I knew I asked him everyday and I knew full well what his name was, Doctor Robert Grey, and he was the nicest doctor in Scapeland Hospital. He was exceptionally nice to me so why I'm not nicer to him I don't know, maybe because I always feel like he's attacking me with all his questions. It put my back up.

"Then why do you ask me everyday what I'm writing? I'm not going to tell you so why do you keep on asking?" I said in frustration.

"Would you like it if I didn't ask anymore?" He paused to wait for an answer then continued "The reason why I ask you everyday is because you never respond to any other question." He paused. " If I didn't ask you about your book we would not talk at all."

His voice rose slightly and he sounded cross. He let out a sigh. "Ok then, how you feeling today?"

I shrugged, I'd said what I wanted to say and I wasn't saying anymore.

"You going to talk to me?" Doctor Grey lent forward on his elbows and held my gaze with his. "If you talk, I can help you. If you want to get better, then tell me what it is that makes you feel you need act this way. What has happened that has made the truth so unbearable?" I looked up at him. What does he know about anything!

The look in my eyes must have told him that the discussion was over. He nodded his head slowly and closed his notebook.

"Right." He said walking across the room and opening the door. "Well, I'll see you tomorrow."

I picked up my pen and paper and stepped out of his office. A feeling of sadness swept over me. That was it now, I wasn't going to see him again until tomorrow, I had no one else to really talk to. The other people here were ok but they were so wrapped up in their own problems. I looked sadly up at Doctor Grey and he smiled down at me and pressed his thumb against my chin. "Maybe tomorrow."

I walked into the communal living room where some of the girls were playing. It was a big room, they had many parties in there and usually the place was buzzing with people. But today it was very quiet. Nearly everyone was outside enjoying the sunshine. I placed my journal on the coffee table and sat down on the nearest sofa to Doctor Grey's office.

I looked around the room. There was Moira sitting on the floor playing snap with Frederick her teddy bear, she's eighteen years old, you would have thought she'd have grown out of that by now. But she was the only survivor in a car accident when she was five. She suffered with a serious head injury and has never mentally matured from then.

There was Kate sitting by the window watching out for Father Christmas, even though it was the end of April. She'd scream out *Ooh I think that was him*. But it would just be a bird or a plane. Same kind of problem with her. Her father sexually abused her for years and then one day she decided enough was enough and pushed him away and he fell down the stairs. Ten years on, he's still in a coma and she's still seven years old. I don't know much about the new girls. There's one girl, Julie. She likes to draw on herself and is forever having baths. You can hear her screams all the way in to the gardens when the nurse is scrubbing at her raw flesh.

I do not really know why I'm here. I have a slight problem with telling the truth, but who doesn't. The main problem comes when I cannot distinguish between lie and truth. A person lies once and then that builds up and becomes so big that some people start to believe in their own lies. The Doctor says I have a slight personality disorder. But in my opinion that doesn't mean I should be in here. I'm not a threat to myself or anyone else. I'm not like these girls, I have a mental age of a nineteen year old, which is pretty good as that is my age. I walked over to the window and patted Kate on the shoulder. She didn't move or even acknowledge me.

"Can I play?" I asked Moira.
She looked up at me and smiled. "Yes please." Came the sweet reply. I sat down and put her teddy on my lap and let her deal the cards.

"Snap." I yelled slamming my hands down on the full deck. "I win again!"

"Oh." said Moira with a puzzled look on her freckled face. "I always win when playing with Fredrick."

"That's because Fredrick is…" I stopped myself before saying he's just a teddy bear. I looked at her deep blue eyes. She was so pretty, she had shoulder length brown hair with a fringe that helped frame her face. It's a shame she is the way she is. "That's because Fredrick is your very special friend and he knows how much you like to win."
She grinned and swooped the bear up in her arms. "You're so clever!" Moira said and kissed his soft furry head.
She was gone now. She could sit there for hours rocking that bear from side to side like a baby. I sometimes wondered to myself, if a bang on the head made her like this then why not give her another whack and maybe she'll snap out of it. But then that wouldn't bring her family back. So maybe it's safer for her to be in her own world. I just wish the doctors could understand that. Just because she's not leading the life they are and acting the age they think she should, doesn't mean it's wrong for her. She should be with a family that will love and care for her the way she is. Not in a cold hospital with a load of 'nutters'.
Julie came running into the living room in a princess Snow White dress, did a twirl and a curtsy. She then lost her balance and fell on the sofa laughing. Kate moved away from the window for the first time that day and sat next to her.

"Do you have one I can try on?" She asked hopefully.

"Sure." Julie said. To my surprise she was American. I went to New York a few years ago and a few exciting memories played in my mind. I watched Julie jump up, take Kate by the hand
and lead her to her bedroom.

"Ooh." Came a squeal of delight from Kate as the creaky wardrobe door opened.
I turned to look at Moira who hadn't even looked up.
I turned the television on. Midday TV was awful. I'd heard some of the girls asking Doctor Grey about getting Sky, I wasn't too sure what that was but anything would be better than this. I looked over at Moira who was still rocking from side to side. I turned the TV up louder and louder to see if she would react, but she didn't even flinch, it was like she wasn't there anymore.

"Turn that down!" Came a harsh voice from one of the nurses.

"Sorry I must have lent on the remote." I turned it off and then realized that whoever turns it on again next will be in for a shock when the sound comes blaring out at them. I just shook my head, the place needs a bit of spicing up anyway.
I walked down the corridor to my room and put my key in the lock, it was stiff and hard to open. I rarely locked my bedroom door because of this reason and noticed that I hadn't today either. I'd asked the nurse to do something about it and they always say it's at the top of their list.
I stepped into my very pink room. Before I had arrived, a very young girl lived in there and everything had to be pink, including food, which came as a problem. I don't know what happened to her.
I sat on my bed and kicked off my slippers. I looked up at my ceiling and laid my head back against my pillow. I am so bored! I thought. I focused on the stain above my head. Dread to think how that got up there. My eyes wondered around the room and then focused on a picture of my late mother on the bookshelf. She was so pretty, a smile that would light up a dark room, black hair streaming over her shoulders and piercing green eyes. I looked just like her, which I liked.

If one didn't know better you would think we were twins. I missed her. She was my whole life. She died recently in a fire. I paused my thoughts and then panicked. "My journal!" I called out, remembering I'd left it in the living room. I slipped my slippers half on and ran out into the cold corridor.

Doctor Grey, who had to hold out his hands to stop me running into him, greeted me.

"Hey, slow down, where's the fire? Forgotten something?" He said kindly holding out my journal.

"I've taken the liberty of giving you some more paper, saw that you where running low."

I took it from him. "You read it?" It was more of an accusation than a question. How dare he read what is not his.

"No I did not, you have not giving me permission to. So I will not read it until I have your blessing." He gave me a reassuring smile and continued. "I have come to see if we're still ok for tomorrow. I thought maybe we could go into the city and get an ice cream together. Not as Doctor and Patient, but as two friends?"

"We allowed to do that?"

Doctor Grey paused and looked at me almost hurt, as if I had insulted him.

"Well, um, I've asked the 'Powers that be' and they said they can't see any harm in a little outing. Might do you good to get out." He put his hand on my forearm and gave it a friendly squeeze. "Goodnight."

"Goodnight." I said softly and watched him walk back down the corridor and out the main doors to the offices at the end.

Ok, I said to myself, sorting out the muddle of papers in my hand. Wow. He had given me a lot more paper. I patted it all together and laid it out neatly on my desk. I believed him when he said he didn't read it. Though I bet he was dying to.

I washed, got into my pajamas and slid into my cool fresh bed sheets. I shivered and rubbed my feet together. I started to write but couldn't stop thinking about the day ahead. I was excited to spend a whole morning with Doctor Grey. I wondered where we would go to get an ice cream, I hadn't had an ice cream in ages. I tried to think back to the last time I had one and what my favorite flavour was, but recently my mind hasn't been able to travel back very far. All I know is what I write down in my Journal. It seems to help me remember.

I've heard people in here say, oh I could never write a journal, and my life isn't interesting enough. But when you sit down and actually think of your past experiences you could be very much surprised.

Even though Doctor Grey taking me out was probably just a ploy to get me to talk to him I was going to enjoy tomorrow. In fact I plan on enjoying every moment.

* * *

I woke up with a jolt and had a clutching sense of fear in my chest. My eyes scanned around my dark room. I could just make out the shape of my wardrobe and chest of drawers.

Far off I could hear screaming. I sat bolt upright in bed. They were screams of pain, I was sure of it. I swiveled round and slipped my feet into my slippers. The scream came again, bellowing down the hall way and seeping under my door into my ears. A twinge of fear took hold of me again and I froze. I felt the little hairs on the back of my neck stand up on end.

The room was cold so I wrapped my dressing gown over my shoulders. I slowly opened my door and stepped out into the even colder corridor. I looked down towards Doctor Grey's office. It was pitch black. I looked up towards the kitchen and I could see a light seeping out under the door. I took off one of my slippers and wedged it between my door and the wall, just in case I couldn't open it.

I stepped forward slowly, there was another piercing scream, which made me jump. I wondered why no one else heard the cries. There should surely be a nurse on night duty. But there was no one around. I got to the end of the corridor and stood facing the kitchen door. I twisted the handle slowly downwards and light billowed out into the hallway. I lifted my arm to shield my face, then slowly I took it down as my eyes adjusted to the bright light. I wasn't in the kitchen. I was in a hallway to what looked like a house, not a very clean one at that. I stepped cautiously into the room. I was astonished to find the place heaving with people, mostly women dressed in the most disagreeable outfits. There were men surrounded by young girls, maybe even younger than I was. The women were kissing the men and undressing them and themselves. Some were mid coitus, others were engaged in the most foul looking foreplay. The place smelt of perspiration, there was a cackling laugh from one of the overly painted girls as a fat man poured his glass of whiskey over her naked breasts.

I heard the scream again coming from the back of one of the rooms leading off from the hallway. I weaved in and out of the naked bodies. No one seemed to acknowledge I was there. I heard the scream again, it was louder and more desperate. In the corner I could see a man bedding a young girl, he seemed to be enjoying it. I walked slowly over to the writhing, sweaty bodies.

I stood in horror when I saw the girl. It was me, lying underneath this big brute of a man, my face twisted in pain and tears were streaming down my cheeks.

I tried hitting the man, trying to get him off but my arms felt weak and limp. I felt helpless. I screamed in frustration as the younger me screamed in pain. All around me people laughed and taunted.

This must be a bad dream, I thought to myself.

"You'll ge' used to i' lav, don' worry."

I heard one of the hookers say, in a strong cockney accent.

"You'll enjoy i' afta a while."

I reached down and grabbed the younger me by the hand and heaved her up, her bottom half was naked and bleeding but I ran with her. Out of the room, past the men and the women and down the long corridor to my bedroom, the slipper was still wedged in my door, I grabbed it and pulled her in. I stood bent over with my hands on my knees to catch my breath

"Are you ok?" I turned around to face her, as there was no reply, but she had gone. I opened my door and looked up and down the corridor. A nurse was sitting at her station reading a book.

"Everything all right?" She asked putting her finger in the place she had stopped reading.

"Did you see a young girl run down the hall just then?"

"No love, sorry."

I thanked her and shut my door.

I felt dirty. I went into the bathroom and started to run myself a bath. I sat on the side of the bath and swirled the water with my hand. Had that been a dream? My legs felt weak and my heart was still thumping within my chest. Doctor Grey had recently been talking about flashbacks. He said I might start remembering things from my past that I may have forgotten. Had that been a flashback? If so I had lived that moment before, and that thought scared me half to death.

Chapter three

The theatre was empty apart from a few players left who were waiting to audition. The five judges were all lined up with pens and paper in their hands, looking very serious, sitting in the middle row.

"Wow, Jennifer you were wonderful!" I said hugging her as I walked through the back stage doors.

"Really, I delivered the lines ok?"

"Yehu! From where I was sitting you did."

"Where were you sitting?"

"Right at the back. I heard every word."

"Oh good." She said sighing with relief and turned to her fans that had gathered to get autographs, when they heard where she was.

"When do you find out about the part?" I yelled over all the chattering of Jennifer crazed men and women. She shrugged and started signing autographs.

Fine, I sighed to myself and stepped out the fire door into the night air. I plunged my hands into my pockets to keep them warm. Jennifer had taken my gloves because she said hers weren't keeping her hands warm, and it could ruin her manicure, apparently.

I looked up at the lamplight towering above my head. There sat a crow perched on the edge ready to take off. It must be a great view from up there, I thought. We were on the bottom floor of our flat and the only view I had was the 'builders butt' belonging to our milkman and that's not a pretty sight to wake up to every morning.

Snow was still falling, it was becoming really deep now. The Gritter trucks were out, trying their best to add some grip to the streets, I think they were fighting a losing battle. They would have probably had more luck asking the weather to stop snowing. I could just see cars creeping along behind one of the trucks trying to get home. Tomorrow will be a total stand still, I thought.

Behind me Jennifer and Jim stumbled out of the door giggling. He flicked her legs up and carried her carefully through the snow.

"I'll make my own way home then." I called up after them as they disappeared around the corner.

* * *

I was right. Sunday morning, I woke up to a world of white. You couldn't see where the pavement ended and the road began. It was so quiet, so still. No cars, no buses just people in big boots crunching through the snow. Most were desperately trying not to slip over. There were some young children building snowmen in the middle of the road.

The Cockney DJ interrupted the song playing on the radio. "It is official, this is the greatest snow fall that England has seen for over 100 years. But get out whilst you can. It won't last long. The sun will be back in a few days and the snow will be gone!"

I looked out at the children playing and thrills of excitement came over me. I quickly threw on my winter warmers and my old jeans and jumper and ran out to the kitchen to get breakfast.

Marie was making breakfast. She didn't look up at me when I entered.

"Where's Jennifer?" I asked dropping some bread into the toaster. "She come back last night?"

With out looking up she replied "No, she stay with thata Jim of ers. 'e nice ha?"

I rolled my eyes and waited for my toast to pop.

"Tis came for you tis morning." She said throwing a book on the table in front of me.

I looked down at it in surprise. It was my book, Escape. Well not my actual book, that was ruined, but this looked brand new. "Who, who sent it?" I asked in shock flicking through the crisp new pages.

"I don'ta know, I'a not a psychic!" She turned around and looked at me for the first time in days, she must have seen the earnest look upon my face.

"A tall man, straighta' black hair, quite nice looking." She said with a smile that could turn your heart to stone.

It was him, the Tall man from Starbucks, the one I spilt my latte on. "Oh my god, how did he get my address?!"

Marie looked at me questioningly. I shook my head dismissively, grabbed my toast and put it in my mouth whilst I put on my coat and boots.

Opening the door the cold hit me like a runaway train. The sun was low in the sky. Across the street children were paying.

"We go' tumora off school!" A small boy called to me from behind a big snowball. He then launched it up in to the air. It came sailing towards me and hit me square in the chest. He giggled and hid behind a half built snowman. I picked up a handful of snow with my bare hands and hurled it in his direction. Unfortunately it broke into a thousand little flakes and didn't even reach half way. The boy burst into laughter and bent down to pick up some more ammunition. But as he stood up a pile of snow was thrust down his neck. He cringed away and threw what little snow he had in his hands at the stranger. The man laughed and stumbled towards me as if he'd been very badly wounded. It was the Tall man from the café. He had a smile on his face like he was some hero who had saved me from the enemy. I smiled back then looked behind him, an army of boys and girls were arming themselves with snowballs.

"Run!" I grabbed his hand and pulled him away from the center of the action. We ran with snowballs belting down our backs.

As we became further out of range the children turned on each other. Their shrieks of laughter could be heard down the street. Still laughing we stumbled into Wimpy and slumped at the nearest free table.

"Think I've got shell shock!" The Tall man laughed.

I breathed a sigh and regained control of myself, suddenly remembering that I didn't have any make-up on and the tall man was sitting right in front of me. I was also wearing the same baggy clothes that I had on yesterday.

"Mmm." I cleared my throat and pointed to the menu. "Breakfast?" He nodded and handed me a menu.

"Thank you for my book, I assume it was from you. How did you know where I live?"

"Don't laugh." He said shyly "But I took your old book out of the bin after you left yesterday, your address was written in the front. Please don't spill Coffee on that one though, it's mine." He added quickly.

"Oh, thank you. I won't. I won't even drink coffee within a five meter radius of it."

We both had a toasted bagel with jam and cream and a nice hot cup of coffee.

"I'm James, by the way." He said reaching over the table to shake my hand. I placed my hand in his and gently shook it.

"Mia." I said with a smile.

"Nice to meet you Mia."

He gulped down his last sip of coffee and reached for the dessert menu. "Ice cream Sundae?"

"*Ice cream,* you are joking?"

"No." He laughed "Believe me, on a day like this an ice cream Sundae is by far the best thing. Cold inside, not so cold outside." He gestured with his head to the door and the snow beyond the thick glass. It made some sense in a way.

"And it's Sunday." He added with a grin.

"Ok, I'd like to have… um, winter berries please."

"Ok, I will have, Christmas pudding." James shut the menu and walked over to the counter.

I quickly took my powder out of my coat pocket and dabbed it on my nose. That should give me a bit of colour I thought and quickly put it away before James took his seat.

"There we are." He handed me my ice cream sundae and looked at me and smiled. The sundae was huge, about the same length from my elbow to my fingertips. "Wow." I said digging my spoon in. "This should make it really warm outside."

He chickled and took a not so gentlemanly mouthful of his and sucked it off the spoon.

"So what do you do?"

"I am a Doctor of hands." He said giving his a wave.

"In what way, Warts and hang nails?" I grimaced.

"Yes, not nice hu? But mostly reflexology."

"Oh Jennifer has that done. But I thought reflexology was done on your feet?"

"It is, but I do it mostly on hands because a lot of my patients don't have feet."

I didn't know quite what to say to that. "I had you down as a Lawyer."

He looked at me with his face screwed up in total disagreement. We both burst into laughter again. I couldn't have been more wrong. I thought back to all those poor people I had labelled with horrible jobs or wonderful jobs that maybe they didn't deserve.

"No, I'm not a lawyer." He sighed. "How about you, what do you do?"

I looked at him from behind my Sundae. "As soon as I tell you this you will know exactly who I am and lose all respect for me. That is if you have any anyway."

He raised his eyebrows and grinned. "I'm intrigued!"

I took in a deep breath and asked slowly. "Bathroom Baby?"

"Oh my god! That's you, you're The Bathroom baby? Jennifer Preston's Daughter? I read all this hearsay about you and you're mum but there's never a full picture of you. There's either the back of your head or the side of your face. You were last in Canada. In… Um."

James looked out of the window as if the answer was out there in the snow.

"Ottawa?"

"Yes that's it. Wow, that's you. I was going to actually ask if you've been travelling because of your accent. Yeah cos' you've been all over haven't you, Wow!"

I had had nothing to worry about. He seemed pretty impressed.

"I'm impressed!" He dug in his long handled spoon to get to the gooey cake at the bottom of his sundae.

"I'm impressed you know so much about me."

He shrugged "A lot of my patients are fans."

"So, you're not a big fan then?"

"I wouldn't say no to tickets to a concert, but not really, sorry."

So he's not that big a fan, I thought. Surprisingly though I liked it.

I had a wonderful time with James. We spent the whole day together. We went to the movies, built a snowman and had another snowball fight in Hyde Park. We made excellent conversation, he talked about work and I talked about all the different places I had been. I taught him a bit of Spanish, he learnt fast. He tried to teach me some points on the hands that signified points on the body, I learnt not so fast. Though he was very patient. Don't give up your day job, he'd said and laughed as I got it all wrong again.

I was falling in love with his laugh. The only men I'd really been around were Jennifer's boyfriends, bodyguards or her agents and they were all very serious men and so wrapped up in Jennifer they didn't have time to laugh or spend time with me. James was serious but he knew how to laugh. He knew what was funny and he'd let you know so. I loved his happiness. It was infectious.

As we approached my apartment I looked up at the seven story high building to the Pent House. We were on the waiting list for that floor. The family that were there at the moment were moving back to America soon and then Jennifer and I will swoop in. I was dreading it. Now we had decided to stay in England she had gone out and bought all this new furniture, like the bath and her new *Electric adjustable king size bed* and more. Now we were going to have to move all that up to the pent house.

"Why do you call your mother Jennifer?" James asked as I put my key in the lock. "Every time you've spoken of her today you refer to her as Jennifer."

"Because that is her name. You want to come in?"

"No thank you. But why, why don't you call her mother?"

"Because she's never asked me to and I've never really wanted to." I looked up at him, he was unsatisfied with my answer. He knew there was more to it than that.

"Everyone around me calls her Jennifer, so that's how I've known her all my life." I paused and thought about what I wanted to say. I took in a deep breath and looked out towards the park. You could just see the Entrance through the thick falling snow. Oh how I longed to forget the question he'd asked and just run through those gates and just keep on running. I stayed staring out at the park. "It, um, it also helps me to keep my distance. She's a very difficult person. She will just cast me aside like an old shoe if she feels like it. So if I don't see her as a mother but as an employer it doesn't hurt me like it should when I do get cast aside or I'm told that she doesn't want me around her at the moment or I'm a waist of space." I looked down at my snow-covered boots and wiggled my cold toes. I felt guilty for feeling that way. It was not natural. All girls have problems with their mothers

but at least in their heart they don't deny that she is their mother. I didn't look up at him. I didn't want him to see my eyes fill with tears. Tears
that had fallen so many times before.
James placed his hand gently under my chin and lifted my head up to look at him.
I blinked and a small tear escaped my eye and ran down my cheek.

"She really bothers you doesn't she."

"I always promise myself that I won't cry any more. But it's hard not to, she's all I have."

"Not any more, if you don't mind I'd like to see you again."
I looked up into his warm brown eyes, he had the slight makings of crow's feet in the corners and they made him look like he was smiling even when he wasn't. Stubble had started to form on his jaw. I followed the lines of hair down to his chin then my eyes focused on his mouth. I could feel his hot breath tingling against my lips. I swallowed hard. "I'd like that." My voice cracked and turned to a whisper. "I'd like that very much."
James tilted his head and bent down to me, I lifted my head higher to meet his lips and closed my eyes. He pulled me into him and kissed me deeply. I was so close, I could feel my heart pounding with in my chest, or was that his heart?
He pulled away slowly and I stumbled towards him, loosing my balance.
I looked up at him and licked my lips, they were moist from his kiss.

"Have a lovely evening." He whispered.

"Good night."

"Buenas noches, Mia."

"Bye." I said quietly and watched him walk away and disappear into the thick wall of snow.

Chapter four

I awoke early the next morning. The sun was already high in the sky and its heat beat down through my open window. The birds were singing their pretty tunes and I could hear some of the girls already laughing and playing in the garden. I sat up wearily and looked around for my journal. I looked down at all the papers scattered over the floor. I must have kicked them off in the night. I slipped my slippers on and gathered them up off the floor. When I suddenly remembered what was happening today, I was going for an ice cream with Doctor Grey. I hurried into the bathroom and had a quick shower.

I put on my best skirt and top, I found my little jacket that was tucked away in the wardrobe and put on my flip-flops that had a two inch heel. I quickly did my hair and make up and admired myself in the mirror. Sometimes when I wanted to I could really dress up like a star. I could smell the toasted Bagels wafting down the corridor from the kitchen. Cook served them up every Sunday.

I sat down with Kate and Julie, who were now the best of friends, they were both wearing princess dresses. Julie had on Cinderella's blue ball gown and Kate had on the Snow White dress with the gold skirt.

"I'm surprised they still do those dresses in your size." I remarked, then kicked myself when I realised what I said. They both looked at me puzzled then carried on chatting with a mouth full of bagel. A new girl came and sat down at our table. I had never seen her before. I looked at her hand holding her coffee cup it was cracked with Eczema and covered in warts.

She caught me looking. "Here you are!" She said, "Have a good look." And thrust her diseased hand under my nose.

I jumped up out of my seat and set my breakfast flying across the table. Kate and Julie grabbed their plates just in time but my full cup of scolding coffee splashed all over poor Doctor Grey who had just entered the dining room.

"Argh!" He exclaimed and stumbled backwards.

"Oh my goodness, I am so sorry." I yelled pointlessly picking up my now empty coffee cup.

Cook came running out with a towel to dry him.

"Don't worry." He said taking his wet jacket off and handing it to Cook, who was fussing over the stained sleeve. "It's too warm for a jacket anyway." He looked at me and smiled. "You ready to go?"

"Yes I'm ready." I said glaring at the giggling girls at the next table. I hadn't finished. I hadn't even started but it was all over the table anyway.

The Warty girl handed me my jacket and smiled. "What a mess!" She smirked and I saw her start helping Cook clear away as we walked out through the glass double doors.

Outside it was humid and there was a taste of honey in the air. The grass and trees were a lush green from the rain the night before and the little brook at the bottom of the garden babbled away.

"Doctor Grey, we going in your car?"

"Yes, that all right?"

"Of course."

He opened the passenger door to his silver Ford Escort. I smiled in thanks trying not to look too excited and slid in.

"Buckle up." He said as he started the engine revs. I reached over my left shoulder and swooped the seatbelt over my chest and clipped it in. I looked down at myself, it made my breasts look huge.

"Ready?"

"Ready." I replied and he sped off down the lane to the Entrance of the Hospital. It seemed like ages since I was last in a car. I couldn't actually remember the last time.

I watched the trees and the houses fly by us as we drove through the streets of London. Boys and girls were playing ball in their front gardens, there were men walking their dogs and skinny women jogging. I used to love jogging, I think.

It was a long drive to where ever we were going and I watched as the beautiful green countryside turned into a city of sky scrappers and very few trees.

"It has been a long while since you were last out hasn't it?"

"No, not really."

"Oh." He said and turned into a busy street.

We parked in a big multi-story car park and he bleeped his key and the car locked.

We went to a little restaurant called Wimpy. It was fresh in there, a lot cooler than the warm air outside, which I appreciated. We sat down at the nearest free table and Doctor Grey past me a menu. "You can have what ever you like." He said opening his.

I looked around. "It's changed since I was in here last."

He looked up over his menu. "When was that?"

"Oh a few months ago. Before I was sent to Scapeland."

He nodded and focused back on his menu. "I'm going to have the summer fruit cake, with strawberries and mint I think, Sundae on a Sunday." He said licking his lips.

"Ooo, that sounds nice! I'm going to have just Summer fruits and ice cream please." I closed my menu and looked up at him.

"Ok." He stood up and went over to the counter. I sat and tapped my nails on the plastic tabletop. I looked out of the window at a scene that I'd looked out on not so long ago. It looked slightly different back then but I couldn't quite put my finger on it. London couldn't have changed that much in a few months, could it?

"Here we are." Doctor Grey snapped me out of my daydream and put my sundae under my nose.

"Yum." I said digging my long spoon in. The ice cream was cold but the fruits were warm. It was lovely.

"So what happened the last time you were here then?"

"I was having breakfast with a friend." I took another mouthful. Partly because it was delicious but mostly so I could take time in answering his next question.

"Who was the friend?"

"Uh a 'riend." I said with a mouthful of pears. Doctor Grey burst out laughing. I covered my mouth to stop myself spitting Sundae all over him. "Just a friend." I repeated after swallowing.

"You come here a lot?"

"I think so."

"What do you mean you think so?"

I glanced over at his sundae and reached over the round table with my spoon. "Could I please try some of yours?"

"Of course." He tilted his tall glass towards me. I motioned mine towards him and he waved his hand to say no thank you. I took a big mouthful. I'm glad I chose what I did, his wasn't half as nice as mine.

"When you came to us we had no record of your existence. No National insurance number, no passport or date of birth. Strange isn't it."

"No." I said coolly. "They must have been destroyed in the fire."

"The fire?" That clearly came as a shock to him.

"Yes, all my belongings were destroyed in a fire. Everything, my clothes, my family. Everything." I looked sadly into my ice cream. It was nearly all gone.

"Your family were killed in a fire?"

"Yes, well my mother was." Doctor Grey fidgeted in his seat.

"I don't know who my father is. I've never met him." I'd never thought about him really. I'd thought of myself as an orphan but he may still be alive.

"So when were you born?"

"June first 1986."

He studied me for a few moments. He wanted to say something, I could tell but it was almost as if he was afraid to.

"What?" I asked with a nervous giggle.

"Do you mind if I write this down?" I rolled my eyes. I knew this was what we would be doing. But I felt so much more comfortable here than in his office that I didn't mind so much. He could ask me almost anything and I'm sure I would tell him. There was just something in the way he looked. The relaxed look he had when he was outside of work, in his jeans and T-shirt. There was something more familiar about him. Upon looking at him, I Suddenly really liked him.

"Please, you see if I go back to work with some information on you they'll let us go out together again."

"You want to go out with me again then do you, Doctor Grey?" I couldn't believe it, I was flirting. Here was a man probably married with children and old enough to be my dad and I was flirting!

He smiled shyly and fetched a mini pen and paper out of his shirt pocket. "Well believe it or not Hilary I like you. Now what is your full name?"

"Hilary Jacobs."

He looked up at me, there was a look of doubt in his eyes. He knew when I was lying but he didn't say anything. "Where were you born?"

"Here in London."

"In the hospital?" I nodded. He'd never believe where I was really born.

"What was your mother's name?" He looked uncomfortable asking the question.

"I don't think you really need to know that." I said more calmly than I felt. "Her name is of no significance as to who I am." He wasn't ready to know who she was.

"Well I do, but don't worry. Do you remember your National Insurance number?"

"No, I don't remember."

"There anything else of the important details I need to know." I shook me head and finished my last scoop of summer fruit sundae. "That's fine, that's the most I've heard come out your mouth in years."

"Years?" I tilted my head and looked at him puzzled.

"Exaggerating." He added quickly and laughed uneasily.

"So what you doing with me on a Sunday morning. Shouldn't you be with your family?"

"Oh my kids are at their mother's house this weekend."

"So you're divorced?" I felt slightly rude at asking but he asked me intimate questions. It's only fair.

"Yes I am, seven years now. We got married at quite a young age. We were young and in love and we enjoyed each other's company. But as we grew older we started to change, we were totally different. Things that used to be important weren't any more. We were looking in different directions, If you know what I mean." I listened intently.

"We both were so caught up in our own jobs and our own lives that we forgot to involve each other in important decisions, like jobs, the home and even our children. The last straw was when she had an abortion without discussing it with me. I was so excited to have another child but she was dreading it. Her argument was that it was her body." His voice started to break. "But it was my baby."

I reached across the table and put my hand on top of his. I could see he was fighting back the tears and to aid his battle he took a big spoonful of ice cream. He sucked in his lips as the cold stung his teeth. He looked up at me, I'd never seen a man look so sad before. Something hung in the air between us, I didn't know what it was but I knew I never wanted it to go. "After seven years it still hurts. She must have really hurt you."

He nodded. He was about to say something else but decided against it.

I looked down and realised that my hand was still on top of his. I quickly moved it away and put it onto my lap. He turned his head and looked out of the window. His eyes wondered around outside, and for a while he was somewhere else.

He turned back to face me and quickly said. "You want to go for a walk in the park?"

I nodded and pushed my empty glass to one side to show I had finished. He gulped down the now milky, creamy mush and stood up.

I followed him outside into the blazing sunshine and shielded my eyes with my hand. He led the way to Hyde Park entrance gate. I turned around half expecting to see a tall building behind me but there was just an empty school.

"You ok?"

"Yeah." I replied, "It's just so different."

"Like you said you've only been away for a few months. It couldn't have changed that much."

"No, I know." A strange feeling came over me, I felt uncomfortable in my own skin.

The park was full of life, children, animals and laughter. I saw a dog barking as his master threw him his ball and he ran like lightening to fetch it. There were people having picnics and playing catch. They were all living their lives so fully in these moments. I looked up at Doctor Grey's kind face. "Maybe one day we can have a picnic here."

"I can't see why not."

I smiled up at him then something caught my eye, a family were sitting on the grassy bank. The parents were playing cards and the two teenage boys were playing rough and tumble. I stared at them for a few moments.

"You all right? You've stopped."

"I recognise that man." I said pointing towards the gentleman playing cards.

"You do?" Doctor Grey said sounding hopeful.

"Yes, I've seen him before. I remember he was very kind to me. He's a lot older now than what I remember but..." I racked my brains. "I think he's a Doctor too." I dropped my head and looked at the lush grass. Who was he?

I then got a flash back. I stood there for a moment trying to piece it together. "I remember knocking on a varnished wooden door then looking up at a metal plaque that read Doctor, and now it's gone, Doctor, Y, O, G. or Y, O, N, G? No that's not right, but it's something like that." I looked up at Doctor Grey with a pained expression.

"You been having many flash backs recently?"

"Yes, at least, I think I have." I explained to him about the 'dream' I had had last night. He listened intently, nodding now and then to show he understood. All the feelings of fear from the experience come back to me. I remembered the state the younger me was in. Blood stained clothes and tear stained face. At the time I thought I grabbed her hand and ran with her, but thinking back I think we were just running away in the same direction.

When I had finished, he stopped walking and turned to look at me face on. He lifted his hand and gently ran the back of his fingers down my cheek and spoke softly, so softly that I had to strain my ears above the screams of laughter to hear him.

"You are so brave. You have obviously been through a lot." He lent closer in towards me, that feeling that had hung in their in air was back again. I was yearning for something but I wasn't sure what it was. He was so close to me that I could smell and taste his sweet breath.

"You're not alone Hilary, I will look after you. I want to look after you."

I could feel my heart racing, was he going to kiss me? Or more to the point was I going to kiss him? Did I want to kiss him? He was so kind and gentle let alone handsome, but does that mean I want to kiss him? Something inside of me was screaming to bring my head up just a little bit and touch his lips with mine. But before I could decide he raised his head and kissed my forehead. I closed my eyes, enjoying the warmth of his breath.

"If I can, would you like me to get in contact with this man if we can work out who he is?" He pointed over to the man lying on the picnic blanket, he was laughing. His laughter filled me with such hope, but hope for what?

"Yes please."

He outstretched his arm and I looped my arm round his.

We walked and talked for what felt like hours. Not long dreadful hours, but interesting conversation full hours. He told me about his children and I told him about my trips to America and Canada and Spain. For the first time in ages, I felt free.

*   *   *

We turned up into the lane that led up to the front of the hospital. He stopped in his parking space and got out, he open my door for me.

"Doctor Grey...?

"Call me Robert, I'd like that."

Robert, I thought. I'd like that too. "Thank you."

"You're welcome."

"Not just for opening the door for me, but for the whole day. I really needed adult conversation. Yes the girls are physically my age but mentally..."

"I know, but the Matron says you're very good with them."

"Well I like them. Apart from that new girl with the warts. She needs to see a doctor about that hand and that temper of hers."

He nodded knowingly. He placed his hand gently on my back and led me up the steps to the main Entrance.

"Ok let's search ya." One of the nurses at the front desk said in a husky voice and reached out for my hand.

"What!" I pulled away from her grasp in discussed and hid behind

Doctor Grey.

"No, there's no need for that." He said coming to my rescue. "I've been with her all day and she has nothing more than what she left with this morning. Except a stomach full of ice cream." I looked up at him thankfully.

"Its regulations!" She protested and went to grab at me again.

"Trust me Miss Synch she doesn't need a strip search. If she has brought anything in here, which I can promise you she hasn't, I will take full responsibility for it."

The semi attractive nurse looked at him then at me and stepped aside.

"I am writing this in my book Doctor!" She yelled as we disappeared into the corridor.

"Miss Synch hu, does that mean she's easy?"

He laughed softly.

"Thank you so much! I was thinking of 'chasing the dragon' tonight but I don't think I will now."

He looked at me puzzled then saw I was joking and laughed again.

"We will do this again."

"Is that a promise or a demand Doctor Grey?" God, I was flirting again.

He lent down and whispered in my ear. "A promise and it's Robert."

Chapter five

"Here." I heard a voice to the left of me say. I turned and a man thrust a newspaper into my hand.

"Thanks." I said puzzled and watched him stumble away through the snow with a bundle of newspapers. I looked down at the evening paper's headline. *Preston Bags Aphrodite.* I can't believe she didn't tell me. You would think being her daughter and her 'main carer' according to Marie, I would be the first to know. But oh no! Everyone else is so much more important. I'm just the shmuck who follows her around everywhere fixing her hair, doing her make up, doing her accounts. Well I quit! No more. She can say what she likes, she can beg and beg she can bitch about me to the papers but this time I will not cave.

"Jennifer Preston, We are through you hear me, through!" I slammed the front door behind me and dumped my coat on the floor and kicked my boots off. "You didn't tell me you got…"

"Where have you been?" She asked as I stormed into the kitchen.

Well someone was with Jim last night. She only ever acts concerned about me after she's climaxed. Well at least she'll be in a good mood for my resignation.

"I..." I started ,but Jim walked passed me before I could answer and she ran to him slightly nudging me out the way. I over dramatically stumbled so she might notice, but she didn't.

"You've been gone for more than ten minutes!" She said and threw herself into his arms.

"Hmph." I groaned, could she act more desperate! That's it, I've lost her attention for the rest of the evening. Even though I didn't have it for a moment. I'll confront her about the matter later but right now I am starving. I opened the fridge door to the huge American Deluxe 3000, but it was empty. I turned around to say there was no food when Jim presented me with ten bags full of shopping and dumped them at my feet.

"Be a doll." He said and twirled Jennifer out of the kitchen into her bedroom.

"Where's Marie?" I yelled as the door closed on me and Marie stepped into the kitchen.

"It is a mi day off." She said grabbing a can of orange juice and some squirty cream out of one of the bags. She grinned that shuddering grin and waltz out. "Enjoy."

I slumped over the bags to find the ones full of the fridge food. But the food was scattered everywhere, mixed bags of fruit and vegetables with the tins. You see when I go shopping I always pack the food away in it's category of food type. Frozen, fresh etc. "Bloody men!" I said out loud as I found the tin of tuna bruising the peaches.

"Ooh, Jimmy." Came Jennifer's shrill voice. I quickly packed the fridge and freezer food away, the tins could wait till the morning. "Oh Jimmy, That's it." I quickly grabbed a packet of crisps and a chocolate bar, pressed them hard against my ears and ran to my bedroom.

My room was on the other side of the apartment and I could still hear them doing it. I looked around my room trying to find something, anything to do. The wallpaper was peeling off my walls and the carpets were crumpling. When we first entered the apartment Jennifer claimed her big room, before Marie and I got a chance. I wanted Marie's room because it was bigger than the one I'm in. But Jennifer said that Marie would be entertaining some old 'friends' and would appreciate the bigger room. Apparently according to Jennifer I have no friends and will be quite happy in the box room. The only good thing about my room was that it overlooked the park. I turned my radio on to try and listen to The Righteous Brothers swooning, and desperately drown out Jennifer and Jim's squeals. I don't know what sought of love making they were doing but half the time they sounded like they had farm animals in there.

"Finally they've stopped. Hu, Jim must be losing his touch."
There was a knock at my bedroom door, I opened it a crack and the hall light streamed into my room.

"Lovey would you please keep it down in here? Jim and I are trying to, you know."

"Yes Jennifer, I know I can hear you. The living rooms between our rooms and I can still hear you. I feel sorry for Marie who's right next door."

"Oh no darling, don't feel sorry for Marie, she's got a fella in her room as well."

"Oh my god!" I screamed and slammed the door.

"So will you keep it down?" Jennifer asked re-opening it again.

"Yes!" I snapped.

"Thanks Hun." She blew me a kiss and shut the door. I listened to her little feet scurry away down the hall and back into her room. "You'd better be oiled up for me Jimmy, cos' you're in for a spanking if you're not!"
I shoved the headphone socket into the radio then the foam plugs into my ears.
It went silent after a while, Jennifer and Jim had stopped or at least

quietened down. I relaxed a bit and took my head phones out of the radio. But then Marie's Italian dirty talk started echoing down the corridor. I heard someone trill their tongue and then a giggle.

"I gotta get out of here." I ran out of my room, grabbed my coat and boots and put them on outside. I couldn't stay in that flat a moment longer. I buttoned up my coat all the way up to my chin. The evening was cold and dark. The light from the street lamp gave the snow that had rested on the ground an orange glow. It was still snowing but more softly now. I stood on the doorstep to our building and looked out over the world of white. The gate to Hyde Park looked as welcoming as ever. I often jogged there when I needed a break from baby-sitting Jennifer. I took in a deep breath and ran as fast as my legs could carry me. I could here my heart pounding in my ears and I could feel it beating hard in my chest. I ran and ran and ran. I was running away from everything. From Jennifer and Jim. Marie and that poor man she had in her room. From the scabby apartment that I had to call home. From the demands and the demands and the demands of my so-called *Mother!!*

My face and hands were freezing and I had a gripping pain in my chest but I just kept on running. My lungs felt like they were going to burst.

I then realised that it had stopped snowing and the little dancing white speckles I could see were in my eyes, like when you stand up too quickly. Apart from the crisps and chocolate I hadn't had anything to eat since breakfast with James and I was really beginning to feel my energy levels dropping. I suddenly got an overwhelming pain shoot up my leg. The world started to spin faster and I could feel myself slowly falling. I heard the snow muffle over my ears and then felt an overwhelming sense of calm take over my body. For the first time in a long while I felt at peace.

* * *

I felt fine until I moved. My legs were aching, along with the small of my back. I raised my hand to the side of my head and felt the big bump that had formed there.

"Ouch!" I opened my eyes and looked up at the ceiling. This wasn't my ceiling. There was a suspicious brown mark just above my head.

"The bath leaks sometimes." Came a deep voice to the left of me. "How you feeling sleeping beauty?"

I gently turned my head on the pillow to find James standing in the door way holding a tray. He looked like an angel. I shrugged my shoulders in response. I didn't really know how I was feeling. "That for me?" I asked, slowly sitting up.

"Careful, you had a really nasty fall. I thought about taking you to hospital but I much preferred the thought of bringing you home to my bed."

"I'm glad you didn't. I *hate* hospitals." I put my entire weight on my weak arms and slowly let myself lean against the headrest.

It was a big room, about as big as the kitchen back at the apartment. It was painted magnolia and a blue, gray. The mouldings on the wall were beautiful and very old fashioned. In fact the whole room was old fashioned. Old chest and wardrobe. Beautiful French windows that opened out to a balcony. I could feel the warmth from the fireplace as it crackled and glowed.

"Wow, I love your room."

"Thank you, here eat this." James handed me the tray. There were piles of pancakes drenched in syrup. A glass of orange juice and one single white rose in a glass of water.

"My goodness, thank you." I picked up the top pancake and tore it in half and took a little bight. James let out a chuckle.

"You must be starving, you can eat like an animal if you want, I won't think any less of you."

I smiled at him gratefully and crammed the whole pancake into my mouth, swallowed and took a big swig of Orange juice.

"God, careful you don't choke to death though."

The bedroom door slowly opened and a little tabby cat slunk into the room and jumped up onto the bed.

"Until now this has been the most important woman in my life." James tickled behind the cat's ear and she moved towards his touch. "Mia meet Penny, Penny meet Mia."

"The only woman until now?" I looked at him questioningly and gave Penny a tickle.

"She just loves pancakes with syrup." He said dodging the question. He broke a little piece off and gave it to her. I was surprised. I didn't know cats were like that. I always thought they were too fussy, unlike a dog who would eat anything.

Penny started nudging James' hand with her head and purred loudly.

"Oh, she saying thank you?"

"No, she's hinting she needs a walk."

"A walk?" I repeated just to check that I had heard him correctly.

"Yes, that's what I was doing Sunday evening when I found you. She won't go out on her own. I think she suffers from slight agoraphobia or something. I even have a special cat lead for her."

"You do? how cute!" I looked down at the paper that slipped off my tray as I shifted in the bed.

"Oh my god!" I said staring at the date. "It's Wednesday! I've been asleep since Sunday?"

"Yes, but don't worry I called your mother, I mean Jennifer and told her what had happened. She said that's fine and said don't worry Marie can do her hair and make up. She didn't really seem to be that concerned."

"Why do you sound so surprised? She wouldn't, it didn't make the papers. Oh my god, Marie doing her make up, She will make her look like a drag queen. She can't even do her own. I'm sorry James but I really have to go."

"Oh no you don't, you are not leaving this bed until that bump goes down."

"But that could take days!"

"That's a sacrifice I am willing to make, I don't care how long you have to stay in my bed, you're not leaving until you are better and before you protest any more I am going to take Penny to the park. So you finish off the pancakes and have a little sleep." He picked Penny up and walked to the door.

"Don't you think I've had enough sleep?"

"Sleeping for days can be very tiring. Listen to me, I'm a Doctor. I always know best."

"Yeah a Doctor of hands." He closed the door behind him. I don't think he heard or he chose not to.

I looked down at the pancakes and licked my lips. "I'm taking no prisoners."

I picked up a pancake in one hand and the newspaper in the other and nearly choked on the mouthful I'd just bitten off. I couldn't believe what I was reading.

"She did what!?"

Chapter six

Robert and I had been to London five times since that Sunday. We'd been out to dinner, at the Hilton Hotel of all places. We met a few of his friends there. He didn't tell them I was a patient. He introduced me to them as *Ms Hilary Jacobs.* They all shook my hand and smiled at me politely. We all made small talk for a while and then they were shown to their designated tables. He'd taken me shopping for new slippers and some clothes, I promised him I would pay him back but he said he wouldn't hear of it, in fact he would be insulted. We had a picnic in Hyde Park just as he had promised. He was becoming more than a Doctor to me, he was becoming my friend. I was now waking up in the morning and looking forward to our meetings. I was talking to him more about my life before I came to the hospital. It felt good to have someone listen to me.

It was Wednesday afternoon and it was a dismal day. The sun seemed to be taking time out for a while. The thunderclouds rolled across the sky like a violent sea. Every now and then the sun would show its face between the breaks in the cloud, but it would go as quickly as it came. I checked my make up in the mirror, I never usually cared what my make up was doing during the day but recently I'd been caring more and more. I retouched my lipstick and put my new slippers on. I put my long black hair up in a French plat and went to the dinning room for lunch. I hadn't seen Robert yet today so I was waiting to be called to his office any minute.

I grabbed a plate and chose a ham and cheese toasty. It was fattening I know, but luckily I've never had to worry about my weight.

I sat down with the now bosom buddies Kate and Julie, they were both having a fish finger sandwich. Kate's Aunt had bought her some princess dresses, so they where both being Cinderella today and were being very careful not to get ketchup down their frocks.

I took a bite out of my toasted sandwich and a big dark figure towered over me then sat down on the chair next to mine. It was Wart girl and she sadly, no longer, just had warts on her hands but, they had spread to her face. She had one on the side of her nose, it seemed to be watching me eat. As slyly as I could I turned my body so I was looking away from it. Things like that really put me off my food.

"What's your *problem?*"

I tilted my head slowly and looked up at her, she was blocking the light coming in through the window so I could only see her fat silhouette. I put my hand above my eyes to try and see her better. "There's no problem." I said timidly.

"Yes there is. You've got a problem with me. I'm sorry if my skin disgusts you." She looked down at me with her tiny gray eyes. "Look at you, you're acting like the cat that got the cream. Just because Doctor Grey takes you out now and then for a nice ice cream you think you're better than all of us!"

"No I don't." I stood up to feel less intimidated but she was still a whole head taller than me.

"Yes you do, well I've got news for you. He's taken me out to Pizza Hut."

"And me for an ice cream." I looked across to the blonde sitting in the corner.

"And me!"

50

"And me!"

"And me!" Soon the whole dinning room was filled with 'and me's.' Even Kate and Julie admitted to him taking them out. I heard a shuffle in the doorway and turned around to see Robert looking quite awkward. I turned back to face Wart girl who had not finished her speech.

"So get off your high horse, you're not special, so stop acting like you are, you old trout!" The room took in a deep breath and all eyes were on me awaiting my response.

"You really wanna know what my problem is with you, do you? You're dirty, spotty, you have got more warts on one hand than a hundred toads." She looked at me shocked. "But do you really want to know what I really can't stand? It's your smell!" I glared at her in the eye, turned and walk out. I nudged Robert out of the way with my shoulder and ran to my room.

I tried my key in the lock but it wouldn't turn, I tried the handle then gave the door a shake. I couldn't open it. In frustration I hit the door with the heel of my hand and a shot of hot pain darted up my arm.

"For god sake!" I lent with my back against my door and slid down so my bottom was on the hard floor. I buried my head in my arms and cried.

I heard a tap on the cold stone floor as feet came towards me. Please walk passed, I pleaded to myself.

"Come on." Came Roberts warm voice from above me. "Up you get."

I looked up at him as he bent down to aid me to my feet. "Are you all right?"

I wiped my nose on my sleeve and dabbed my eyes with the back of my hand.

"Here."

I took the hanky he offered and softly blew my nose. "Why are you sitting out here?"

"My, my door won't open."

He grasped hold of the key in the lock and tried to turn it. He struggled for a moment then the door popped open.

"Thanks." I said not even looking at him and turned to go into my room, my sanctuary.

"Hey," He said clutching my elbow and gently pulling me towards him. Looking at me very seriously he said. "Only once have I taken those girls out and that's when they first arrived. To make them feel comfortable so it's easier for them to talk to me. But you I've taken out more times than I've been allowed." His voice sounded desperate. He stopped short to regain control of himself.

"Please let go of my arm!" I demanded, before he could say anything else.

He was now holding me quite tightly. He looked at his hand and slowly released his grip, then let his arm drop. "You have no idea how special you are do you!"

"Well according to Wart girl I'm not special at all." I sniffed and looked at him. "See you in our meeting Doctor Grey."

"Please Hilary talk to…"

But I didn't let him finish I walked in and closed the door. I walked across the room and sat on my bed trying to fight back the tears.

"Matron, get someone in to fix this door!"

I heard him say in the assertive tone he uses when he wants something to be done, no questions asked.

I picked up my pen and paper and began to write. I paused in my thoughts and thought back to the confrontation I had just had in the dinning room. What on earth did she mean 'Old trout.' I was not that much older than she was. She couldn't be more than sixteen. I decided to put it to the back of my mind and not think of it again. I was tired and my eyes felt swollen from my tears I put the lid on my pen and sunk my head into my pillow.

*   *   *

I felt a pain in my groin. A cramping and gripping pain. I could see hundreds of different faces whirling and swirling around me, I wanted to scream out, but I couldn't. I looked down at myself, I was covered in blood. I could hear women's screams and men's shouts but I could not work out what they were saying. Then in a swirl of mist Doctor Grey's face appeared above me and smiled.

"It's going to be ok." His face was so close to mine but his voice was so far away.

There was another excruciating pain and then it was over. I felt wet. Doctor Grey handed me something rapped in cloth. I took it and cradled it in my arms. Then another man who I didn't know came and took the bundle away. I held on tight but he was too strong. I clawed and reached to try and keep what ever it was but I was too weak.

"No!" I screamed out.

I woke with a jolt. I sat up in bed and looked around. I was back in my room. The bed covers were gathered up around my waist where I must have been pulling on them. It was dark. I didn't know how long I had been asleep. I heard some one struggling to open my door and the nurse burst in. She was relieved, I think, to see I wasn't dead. I was sweating and panting. I looked down and my bedclothes, they were soaked, I had wet myself.

"Oh god I am so sorry. That is so embarrassing!"

The nurse helped me out of bed. "Don't worry dear. It's happened before. I'm just glad you're ok. You gave me quite a fright." She started stripping the bed whilst I went into the bathroom to change and run myself a bath. I sat on the lid of the toilet and wrapped my legs up in my arms. What a horrible dream. I still felt uneasy and upset. I wonder what could have been wrapped in the cloth. A baby? The nurse interrupted my thoughts and knocked on the bathroom door. "I'm going to have to tell Doctor Grey."

"Oh please don't." I pleaded wrapping my gown around me so I could open the door. The nurse stepped back.

"You know I have to tell the Doctor. If it's a problem him knowing, for any personal reasons, then I'm sure the Governor would be very interested to hear about it." The nurse gave me a knowing look and waited for my reply.

"No, tell him." I closed my eyes and shook my head.

"Only because he will need to write it in his report." She tried to justify.

"It's ok. Just tell him." I looked at my fresh clean bed. "Thank you for doing that."

She walked towards the door and ushered the girls away that had gathered to find out what had disturbed them. Wart girl was one of them and she gave me a sarcastic wave as she was escorted out of theroom.

"I'll leave this open, just a little bit. Call if you need me." The nurse shut the door behind her but not enough to make it click. I wasn't bothered I just wanted to wash the urine off my legs. I stepped into the bath and slowly sat down. I reached over for my headphones so I could listen to the radio and sunk my shoulders into the warm water.

After drying myself I walked over to my bed and reached under my pillow for my pyjamas, they weren't there. The nurse must have taken them with my bedding. I walked over to my chest of draws to get out another pair. I sat on my bed still feeling shaken up about the dream. I hate nightmares, I always find it's really hard to get back off to sleep afterwards. I'm always worried, I will have that same dream again. I reached over to my bedside table where I had left my journal. I couldn't feel it. I turned my head to look, I looked under my book then in the draws. I let out a sigh of relief when I found my papers in the bottom draw. I fished through to find where I last left off, but it was just a pile of blank sheets. I looked up in panic. The nurse wouldn't have taken it. She would have had no need. I thought back. Had I taken it out of my room today? No I hadn't. I got out of bed and started rummaging through my draws in my desk then I looked under my bed. Now I was starting to really panic. This was my life I had lost. All my life was written on those sheets of paper. I ran to the door and stopped in my tracks, it was open. I heard the nurse say she would not close it in case I needed her. Someone unwelcome had been in my room and had taken my Journal. I flung the door open and ran out into the cold hall. I asked the nurse on duty if she had seen someone go into my room.

She shook her head. "Not since the nurse, though I was away from my desk a few moments to go to the toilet. But only for a few moments, not long."

"Argh." I screamed in frustration. "Someone, whilst I was in the bath, came into my room and stole my journal."

"Why would anyone want to steal your journal?"

"Are you calling me a liar?"

"Well, it says"

"Forget about what it says. Look, this is important to me."

"You've done this before Hilary." Said an older nurse who had just stepped up. "Losing something, then blaming someone else. Making a big scene to get attention, and after what happened in the dinning room today…" She shrugged.

"That's it." I said ignoring her remark. "She did it, that bitch!" Remembering Wart girl standing at my door.

"Now come on. Back to bed. Everyone is asleep, nothing can be done tonight." Said the first nurse. She put her arm around my shoulder. I shook it off and started screaming.

"You're not listening to me. That Wart girl has my journal, she's going to read it."

"Wart girl, what are you talking about? Look, if you don't calm down we'll call security."

The two nurses held my arms.

"Let me go." I screamed rearing about and kicking my legs. "I have to get it back." Then out of the corner of my eye I saw Doctor Grey appear through his office door.

"Oh Robert!" I screeched, "You'll believe me."

He marched up. "What's going on?"

"She's out of control!" The nurse struggled to keep me in her tight grasp.

"No I'm not!" I screamed lurching myself away from them. "If you just let go!" But by pulling again I scratched one of the nurses arm.

"She drew blood!" I heard her exclaim.

"Ok. I'm sorry Hillary."

I looked at him then saw what he was holding. "No!!!" I screamed, struggling to get away but it was no good the nurses were too strong. I felt a sharp pain in my leg and my body slowly went limp. I felt the nurses loosen their grip but I couldn't move. I felt like I was falling. My eyelids were getting heavy and I couldn't keep them open no matter how much I fought against them. I looked up the corridor and saw Wart girl smirking at me in the door way to her room. The hall was swirling round me. Some more girls stepped out into the corridor to see what all the noise was. I felt like I was in a fish bowl looking out at all the faces. Then I saw nothing but blackness. I was left with anger but no way to fight it. Then, nothing.

Chapter seven

"What on earth were you thinking?" I screamed down the phone. "How dare you get married with out me being there Jennifer? I always go to your weddings I'm your daughter for god sakes."

"That's why I didn't think you would mind, this is my third, and you went to the other two."

"Well how do you think it made me look? The uncaring daughter who doesn't go to her mothers wedding." My voice was shaking, not just from anger but I was only wearing knickers and one of James's T-shirts and the hallway was freezing.

"Oh darling don't worry about that, no one noticed you weren't there. Anyway I thought maybe Marie would like to be chief bridesmaid this time. There are lots of photographs."

"Marie? But she's ugly. Why on earth would you want her as a bridesmaid she's just a maid?"

"Now, now Mia that's not a nice thing to say and she wasn't a bridesmaid, she was my maid of honour. Quite fitting really. And she's *not just* my maid, she's a good friend. And the press loved it. Showed I have a compassionate side."

I'd never hated that woman as much as I did right then.

"Well I'm glad your image is still top notch!" I said in a sarcastic manner. "I didn't even know you were getting married so soon. I thought you where going to wait until the spring."

"But the winter's so beautiful don't you think? Especially as it's been snowing."

"It doesn't matter what I think any more Jennifer. Because I quit!"

"Oh don't be petty child, you're not quitting."

"Oh yes I am Jennifer, this time I really am."

"Really, for good?"

"Yes, for good." I don't think I ever sounded so assertive.

There was a pause and then a reply I thought I'd never hear come out of her lips.

"But Mia, I, I need you. I can't, I can't do this with out you." Her voice sounded frail, she sounded like she really meant it. My heart went out to her. She made hating her so easy for me to do, but loving her was even easier.

Her voice echoed down the phone line. "Please don't leave me to do this on my own." For the first time in her life she didn't sound like some fabulous Broadway star. She sounded like a really person who was in the middle of having their heart broken and I was the one doing the braking, I was bringing this suddenly frail lady to her knees and it felt criminal.

I swallowed the lump that was rising up in my throat. No she wasn't going to manipulate me. If this was a ploy to get me to stay it won't work. "Well you're not on your own now are you, you have Jim and Marie." I said sternly.

"Yes that's right, I do." She said softly. "Well I'll see you soon, bye." The receiver clicked and the line hummed dead. I stood still for a moment or too, motionless with the phone still to my ear listening to the gentle hum. I was shaken out of my trance when the latch on James' front door clicked open and he and Penny burst into the hallway along with a gallon of snow drifting in behind him.

"Hey I thought I told you to..." He stopped short as I turned around to look at him. "Hey what's wrong you're as white as a sheet." I opened my mouth to reply but no words came out. He looked strait at me then his eyes fell downwards to my half naked body. He looked uneasy and took his long coat off and wrapped it round me.

"Why don't you have a bath. You must be dying for a nice long soak." He led me to his bathroom and started running the hot water. He squeezed in some bubble bath and I watched it foam under the stream of water. "How do you like your baths, really hot?"
I nodded in response.

"Look, whatever it is I'm sure it's not as bad as what happened out there this morning."
I looked up at him.

"This poor women was walking along in the snow and must have stood on some black ice or something, she flipped up in the air taking the newspaper stand with her and landed with her skirt over her head. Tell you what, today was not a good day for going commando. You could see everything."
I giggled slightly at the poor women's misfortune.

"And then, just to top off the women's embarrassment another woman's, little girl shouted out at the top of her voice, hey mummy yours is like that." He clapped his hands together and burst out laughing, like he'd been holding it in the whole time.

"Why wear no knickers on a day like this?" I couldn't help myself but laugh too. "I've quit." I said sounding serious again.
He stopped laughing and looked at me.

"What do you mean you've quit? Quit what?"

"Jennifer and I are finished, I've quit. No longer doing her hair and make up. No longer being on beck and call every second of the day. If she wants that she can hire a professional. But I will not being doing it any more."
James looked at me not quite knowing how to respond. "I." He let out a little sigh and put his arms around me, in a big bear hug. "Are you

59

happy with that decision?" I looked up at him, into his deep brown, green eyes. You could get lost in there I thought. His breath was warm and I looked at his lips. I wanted to kiss him. My heart pounded in my chest. I was worried he would feel it.

"I think so." I said braking away from his embrace.

"Is this because of her getting married without you?"

"Yes, but don't worry, people didn't even notice that I wasn't there." I said sarcastically.

"I bet they did. Look I think you're perfectly right to be angry, and maybe it is time you found a job of your own. Stand on your own two feet."

He was right. I'd never had a job. Yes Jennifer paid me for what I did, but not half as much as she would a professional. "That's why she sounded upset when I said we were through." I said out loud. "She's gonna have to pay someone big time to do all the jobs I used to do."

"No, I'm sure it's because she knows you're serious this time and she has lost you as an employee."

I hope so, I thought

"Here we are." He said swishing the cold in with the hot. "That ok?"

I put my fingers into the warm welcoming water. "It's perfect."

He grinned and opened the door to leave.

"No stay, I don't want to be alone. Be nice to have someone to talk to."

He looked at me thoughtfully then nodded. "I'll turn around so you can get in."

I took off his coat and shirt and slipped off my knickers. I tested the water again with my toe, It was just right. I then slid my body in.

It was a big corner bath set bellow the floor level so you had to step down into it. It was beautiful with old fashioned taps in the middle on the side against the wall. A bath definitely made for sharing.

I swished the bubbles up so they were covering my chest. "Ok I'm in."

James slowly turned around and walked over to sit on the chair that was facing me. "So what are you going to do?"

"Could I please stay here for a while longer? I'll pay my way obviously. I just really…"

"Hey Mia, you can stay for as long as you like and don't worry about giving me money. I don't want to blow my own trumpet but I earn more than I know what to do with."

"Well as soon as I find another job I'll get my own place."

"No rush. Penny and I like having you around, even though you have been asleep most of the time. I liked coming home to see how you were doing. Actually I looked forward to it." He smiled shyly.

"Thank you." I looked at him and held his gaze.

He fidgeted in his seat. He was a grown man but he looked like a little boy very much aware that I was naked.

"I'm gonna go."

"No don't." I reached out to him and the bath waved. He turned his head so as not to see me.

"Get in with me. I'm sure it's big enough for two."

"I don't know if it is, I've only ever bathed by myself." He looked over at the door.

I suddenly felt sorry for him. "If you don't want to that's fine, I won't be insulted." I said softly.

"No, no I do want to…" He protested "But…"

"But what?"

"Nothing." He shook his head, thought for a while then gradually started to unbutton his shirt. His chest was smooth and shapely. Just as a chest on a man should be, I think. He had a trail of hair running down over his stomach and around his tummy button. He looked at me before taking off his boxer shorts.

"You want me to turn around, sorry!" I turned my head and waited for the soft sound of his boxer shorts as they hit the floor. I bit my lips together. This was unknown territory, scary and unnerving. But I liked it.

I felt the water rise as he slowly slid in. "Ok?" I turned my head back to face him and relaxed my shoulders.

His bathroom reminded me of the bathrooms we had in France. Around the lower half of the walls were wooden slats painted white. The windowsill was a sea blue and he had a little lighthouse ornament placed in the centre. There was a hanging basket above the toilet, filled with blue and white flowers that I did not know the name of. The floor was wooden and also painted white. You could just see the colour of the wood coming through where it was worn. The whole room looked very rustic.

"Oh it's so nice to be able to relax."

"Are you not allowed to relax at home?"

"No, don't be so silly! Only Jennifer is allowed to relax. She'll relax whilst I worry about the accounts or sorting out problems that she has with her agent. You know, she would get into the bath and leave the bathroom door unlocked, so I'd go in, unknowing she's in there to use the toilet and she'd say *oh love whilst you're in here could you rub my back, I'm so stressed.* She never gets stressed, ever. No she leaves that to me, I just, I just, god I'm not even there and she's making me angry."

"No you're not there, you're here with me, and you are staying for as long as you like." He beckoned me over to go and sit near him. "Come here and I will rub *your* back."

I slipped across the bath and turned around so I was facing away from him. I felt his warm wet hands on my shoulders as he pulled me closer to him. He had lovely strong hands and he added pressure to all the right places. I felt my body relax under his grip. "That feels really good."

"Thank you. Hands are different to backs obviously but it's the same idea." After a while he become more gentle and started stroking along my neck and down my shoulders. I felt his hot breath on my cheek and he gently pressed his lips against my neck.

I felt my heart twang and excitement tingled in my stomach.

He slowly kissed down from my ear and over my shoulder. I let out a pleasurable moan. He placed his hand underneath my chin and turned my head so we were lip to lip. He parted my lips with his tongue and kissed me deeply. He pulled away and looked at me. I smiled and he kissed me again harder this time and with more passion. I moved around so I was facing him. We kissed passionately for a long time. He moved one of his hands from around my shoulders and down to my breasts and massaged me gently. In response I moved my hand slowly down his body. Over his chest and followed his hair downwards but he stopped me. Gently raising my hand up out of the water. "No, not in here." He smiled. "Come on." Still holding my hand he stepped up out of the bath. He reached for his big towel off the heated towel rack and wrapped it around the both of us.

The house did not have central heating because of its age so it was freezing.

I shivered and pushed my body closer to him to keep warm. He looked at me like he had a sudden idea. "Wait here!" He said. Leaving the towel with me, he streaked across the landing to his bedroom.

Penny was sitting in the hall and followed him with her eyes. She then looked at me and tilted her head.

"Right, where were we?" He said running back to me and lifted me up so I could wrap my legs around him. He pressed my back up against the wall and kissed me hard. He then carried me to his bedroom. The curtains were drawn and the fire was lit. He laid me down on his bed and kissed my breasts. He worked his way down slowly, kissing every contour of my body. The room danced with the flames from the fire and everything light up, seemed to flicker along with my racing heart.

"You are so beautiful."

"Thank you." I replied. No one had ever told me I was beautiful before. I kissed him hard on the lips and before I knew it we were making love.

Chapter eight

Far away I could hear a clock ticking, its gentle rhythm cranking through my brain.

I felt like I was swimming through a sea of glue, reaching forward for something, anything to hold on to stop me from drowning. But there was nothing. I was on my own in a sea of nothingness and the glue was sucking me in, down and down till it was over my mouth and nose. Its thick substance was suffocating me. Before my eyes disappeared under its surface I saw Doctor Grey shout something and he reached out for me, pulling me up until I had left the glutinous sea.

"Hilary, Hilary you're all right!" I heard him say. "Hilary, you're ok." Everything went still and I could hear the tap of shoes and the rustle of papers. My eyes opened a slit and bright light welcomed me back to consciousness. I tried to focus and could just make out a lampshade. I felt nauseous and my head was pounding.

"Hilary? Hey welcome back." I felt him take my hand. At first I felt receptive. But then a flash of what had happened the night before shot through my mind and I moved my hand away.

"How you feeling? You're in the hospital ward. Just so the nurses could keep a closer eye on you. You feel hungry?" I felt him reach over my bed and then what felt like a tray rested on my knees. I bit my lips together. My vision was blurred but I could just make Doctor Grey out. I turned my head and looked away from him.

"Ok, well if you start to feel hungry your food is there and if you need some help, just press this."
I felt him put a small plastic object in my hand and he closed my fingers around it. The bed rose up as he left. I heard his feet stop so he must have looked back. But I had turned completely on my side with my back to him so I couldn't see.

"Keep an eye on her." I heard him say and then the sound of his shoes clicked away and out of the room.
I curled up into the foetal position and buried my wet cheeks into my blanket. I was crying, how dare he betray me then think he can be my friend again, just like that. He should have listened to me. He's supposed to be my psychiatrist. Isn't that what they do, listen! I then remembered my journal. That bitch must still have it. I slowly lifted myself up to a sitting position. My head was spinning like I'd been partying all night. Oh how I wished that really was the reason as to why I felt so awful. I looked down at my hand where he had placed the buzzer. I pressed it with my thumb, even that took a lot of effort. A few moments passed and a slightly dishevelled nurse came waddling in, trying to flatten her ruffled pencil skirt.

"Yes?" She said and looked at me as if I'd interrupted her very important life and she had no time for whatever it was I had to say.

"Um, has anything happened about my journal, anyone found it?" I asked timidly.

"No, no one has found any journal, or anything of that kind. Doctor Grey searched your room to see if it's in there and asked the other girls and they claim they knew nothing of a journal. Just that you write a lot, but have seen nothing."
I nodded in response and looked down. I felt heart broken. I imagined

Wart girl reading it and laughing at my inner deepest thoughts. My whole life spread across her bed, exposed to such a horrible unworthy creature. I breathed out hard. Trying to hold back the tears. I didn't want to cry in front of the nurse.

"Is that everything?"

I looked up at the impatient woman and could see she wanted to go back to who ever she was 'doing' in the nurses' cupboard. I shrugged and she scurried away quickly. I heard a door click shut and a key turn in the lock.

No one cared, they probably didn't even believe me. I tried to swallow the growing lump in my throat and bent forward to reach my food. It was a tray of four tuna sandwiches, a chocolate bar, an apple and some grapes and a carton of fresh orange juice. I was very hungry and pleased to have such a feast. I put the tray on my lap and started with the sandwiches. I looked over at the clock on the wall, realising that I was completely disorientated. I didn't know the time or the date. How long had I been asleep? It was 12.45 by that clock, but no date.

I finished my lunch and put the empty tray by the side of my bed. Strangely I felt very tired. I snuggled back down in the blankets and tried to get the worries of my journal out of my mind.

I woke up with a start as I felt something hit my leg. I turned to see Doctor Grey standing beside me.

"Sorry." He said, " I didn't mean to startle you."

"You didn't." I lied.

"The girls know you're awake and send their love."

Sure, I thought, they're just upset I'm not dead, Vultures.

"This came for you, someone dropped it off at the front desk." He passed me a gray cloth bag that he rested on my leg. I took it and looked at him, waiting for him to leave.

"I'll go." He said taking the hint. I watched him leave then looked down at the bag. It looked handmade, quite poorly made if you ask me. I read the label, it had the address of the hospital and then my name. It didn't have a stamp so it must have been hand delivered. A shudder of excitement came over me. I didn't know many people. I didn't have a clue who it could be from. My excitement got the better of me and I pulled the drawstring and opened the bag.

I couldn't see what was inside, the bag was thick so it wasn't letting much light in. I reached my hand in and felt around. I pulled out some bits of scrap paper. That must be to protect what ever it was inside. I could feel a lot of soft materiel but nothing solid. Puzzled I reached for my breakfast tray and took off my empty plate and carton. I lifted the bag up and carefully poured its contents onto the tray. I flattened the bits of papers, they were burnt, but apart from that there was nothing. I looked back into the bag to see if what ever it was had sunk to the bottom. It was empty. I then stopped and looked back at the pile of papers on my lap. I picked up a piece and lifted it to the light. I could see some words written in my handwriting. I picked up another, the same, and another.

"NO!" I screamed. I slid my legs out from under the tray and stood on the cold hard floor. "Doctor Grey!" I didn't take my eyes off the pile of ashes on the bed.

"What is it?" He said panicking. "I heard you scream." He stopped and looked at me, then followed my eyes. He picked up a big piece and read out loud. "Sunday morning and I woke up to a world of white, you could." He stopped and looked at me. "This is your journal!"

My eyes filled with tears. When I entered the hospital this was the only thing I had with me. My only possession. The only thing in this god damned world that belonged to me. Doctor Grey placed his hand on my shoulder and pulled me into him. He wrapped his arms around me tightly as I wept. I put my arms around his waist and gripped onto his shirt. I didn't want him to let me go for fear that I may fall.

"Just put them back in the bag and take it to my office." He ordered the nurses. I heard the rustle of the papers and I wept even more. He held me tighter as if *he* was scared to let me go. "I feel like I've failed you. I should have listened to you." He squeezed me harder. "Come on." He said and led me out of the ward. We walked down the long corridor then turned a corner and he unlocked the door to a room. With his arm still round my waist he led me in and shut the door behind us. I wiped my eyes and looked around. We were in a kitchen.

"Where are we?" I sniffed.

"This is where I live."

I tried not to look shocked.

"I live here during the week then I go to my house in the country at the weekend." He flicked a switch and the kettle started to boil. He gestured to me to go through another door into his living room. It was very minimalist. No pictures on the wall just a two-seat sofa a TV and a plain square white table with two chairs.

"You only entertain one person at a time then?"

"Three's a crowd." He shrugged then smiled. "Tea or coffee?"

"Coffee please, two sugars."

"Milk?"

"Yes please." I walked over and sat down on his sofa. The place was very clean and fresh. There was another door in the opposite room. I assumed was his bedroom.

"Here we go. It's hot so be careful."

I smiled in thanks and took the steaming mug from him. He was right it was hot. The knuckle at the top of my middle finger touched the porcelain and made me jump. I blew into the brown liquid and watched it ripple. Then looking past my coffee cup and saw that I was still wearing my silk pajamas and no bra. Feeling self-conscious I crossed my legs and fitted my arm under my breasts to hoist them up a bit.

"You want to talk about it?"

I shook my head then said. "I hope Wart girl gets severely punished for what she's done!"

"So much for not wanting to talk about it. Look we can't punish Chloe until we are sure she did it."

"Yes well, I know *Chloe* did it."

He tilted his head and raised one eyebrow.

"You can't prove that Hilary, don't go out and just accuse her because it could cause even more trouble."

"What, like the trouble and *pain* she's caused me!" I felt my blood start to boil and my eyes fill up with tears as I began to think back to the moment in the ward

"She's in here because she's severely suicidal and has a slight personality disorder, she's very sensitive."

Under usual circumstances I'd feel sorry for her. But I didn't, not a twinge of sympathy.

Doctor Grey took a sip of his coffee. He was fidgeting in his seat and he looked like he was chewing over something. Like there was something he really wanted to say.

"What is it?" I asked eventually. "You look like you're going to pop."

"Ok." He said suddenly, taking me aback. "Will you promise not to get angry with me if I show you something?"

"Well that depends on what it is."

"No, you must promise not to get angry. What I've done could be unforgivable."

I looked at him thoughtfully. His dark hair had a tint of gray in it which was very sexy. He had smile lines around his mouth and laughter lines around his eyes. But there was such wisdom in there. He wasn't that old, late thirties maybe, but it looked like he'd seen so much of life already.

"Ok." I said slowly. "I promise no matter what it is I will not get angry." I put my three fingers up above my shoulder. "Scout's honour."

He laughed nervously. "Wrong arm."

I quickly changed coffee cups over from one hand to the other and raised my other hand up in the air. "Promise."

He looked hesitant.

"Please just show me. Unless it is *literally* a skeleton in you're cupboard I can't imagine it being that bad."

He stood up and walked over to some drawers that were hidden behind his television. He pulled out a blue folder and set it down on the coffee table next to me. He then took my half drunk cup of coffee out of my hand and placed it beside the folder. I looked up at him and he bent down, took my hands and pulled me to my feet.

"You know," He stopped short and pondered for a while. "Before you see what's inside there I want you to know something, something I really shouldn't be telling you." He looked away, he seemed in pain. I wanted to comfort him. My heart started to pound in my chest from nerves and excitement. He fixed my gaze with his and I couldn't pull away, I didn't want to pull away.

"You see once you know what's in that folder you'll probably hate me."

"I could never hate you." I whispered. I stepped in closer to him. I could feel his warm breath on my forehead.

He swallowed hard. "I like you above all others. You're the only patient here that I see every day. I only really need to see you three times a week. I love being with you, I love how you always look so pleased to see me, even if you've only just left my office."

My heart was really pounding. I swear he could hear it. "Well I *really* like you."

"You do?"

"Yes, I only tell the truth when I'm with you, I don't feel I need to hide."

"Really?" Before I could question the questioning tone to his voice he continued. "Well there's only one thing for it." He let go of one of my hands and reached for the blue folder. He handed it to me and stepped back to give me room.

I opened the flap and pulled out a handful of papers. It was my journal.

"I didn't read it." He said quickly. "I always keep a copy of every document I make and as you're not allowed to use the photocopier I..."

I dropped the folder on the floor and flicked through the papers. Everything was there. My eye's filled up with tears and my body shook. It felt like my life had been given back to me. I looked up at Doctor Grey who stood with his hands in the prayer position pressed against his lips. I suddenly felt like screaming and jumping up and down with excitement. I ran and jumped up into his arms and flung my arms around his neck.

He held me as if I weighed no more then a leaf.

"Thank you so much!" I bent my head and kissed him on the lips. I pulled away quickly realising what I had done. He lowered me to the ground and I stepped back feeling very embarrassed. "Well thank you so much, I'd better be getting back, they'll be wondering where..." Before I could finish Doctor Grey grabbed me and kissed me. A full strong kiss on my lips, he gently pushed his tongue in my mouth and I gratefully received him, massaging his tongue with mine. I dropped my journal as he picked me up and thrust me against the wall. It hurt my back slightly but I didn't care. My body started to yearn for him. He stopped kissing my mouth and moved down massaging my neck with his lips. I lifted my head and let out a moan. I gripped his hair and moved his head back up so I could kiss him again.

He let go of my legs and I gently dropped to the floor. I had to tilt my head up to kiss him. But he pulled away.

"I'm sorry." He walked across to the other side of the room. "I'm taking advantage of you."

"No you're not, God no." I stepped forward. "Don't say things like that, you'd never take advantage of anyone, let alone me."

"We can't do this. You're doing too well in our meetings for me to ruin it all." He put his fist against his forehead. "You must go."

"No." I said firmly. "You can't make me fall in love with you and then..." I stopped. I closed my eyes and turned away from him, shocked with what I had just revealed. As I turned I knocked over his waist paper basket. It rocked side to side for a moment until it tipped over, spilling it's contents onto the floor. I bent down to pick up the crumpled paper.

"Leave it." He whispered, "You, you're in love with me?"

"No." I said looking down at the floor.

"I didn't mean to make you fall in love with me." He said quietly. "Look Hilary, if they find out about us they will move me to another ward, they're already suspecting something. I'm treading on thin ice here."

"Well I'd hate for you to loose you're job." I bent down and collected my journal that had been sprawled across the floor.

"Hey don't be like that." He said helping me.

"No, you don't be like it!" I glared at him and took the papers from his hand.

"Thank you for doing this for me. It means a lot. May I?" I said motioning towards the folder.

"Yes keep it." He said sadly.

I picked it up off the floor and headed out the door. I glanced back before I closed it and watched him sink into the sofa with his face in his hands. I wanted to run over and cradle him in my arms. But he was right. Whilst he was my Doctor there was no hope of us ever being together.

Chapter nine

I looked over to the small bedside table, at the alarm clock. It glowed red and the digital numbers read 21:00. I looked down at James who was resting his head on my chest. His dark hair was incredibly soft and I liked running my fingers through it. I looked down at his torso, the fire made the shadows of his masculine chest dance as he steadily breathed in and out.

I'd never been in love before, I didn't know how it felt. All I'd seen of love was from watching films and reading books. If I had a pen and paper right now I would write about this very moment. Because stories last forever and I hoped that this feeling would as well.

"Have you had many lovers?"

"What?" James looked at me puzzled. "Have you had many lovers?" I repeated.

James cleared his throat before he spoke. "No, not really. I've only really had one serious relationship and that last for three years."

"What happened?"

"She cheated on me. She was seeing another person for the last year we were together."

"Oh." I said, and then thought, "Person?"

"Turned out she liked women more than men. She left me for her."
Wow, I really didn't know what to say to that. First I expected him to have more relationships than that, and second I would never have thought his only girlfriend was now gay. "Well I didn't expect that."

"Not many people do." He looked sad and I wished I had not asked. I lifted his head and kissed him. He moved on top of me and we made love again for the third time that evening.

* * *

The phone rang for the fourth time that morning. James was fast asleep and didn't hear it. Whoever it was must really need to talk to him. But I didn't dare disturb him, he looked beautifully peaceful. I could always take a message.

I looked over at the clock. 07:30, who'd be calling this early?

I got up and put his dressing gown around me, I reached the phone just in time.

"Hello?"

"Mia?" Jennifer's voice came trembling down the phone. "Come back, please Mia. Look you've made you're point now. Come home. I need you."

"Hello Jennifer." Not sounding very thrilled to hear from her.

"Please, I need you. It's been days since I last saw you." She pleaded again.

"No you don't need me Jennifer. Well not in the way you should need me."

"Yes I do."

"No. You just need me to tell you how wonderful you are and how much the world loves you." I quickly lowered my voice as I was shouting. "Look Jennifer I've told you, James is letting me stay with him and I'm happy here. I'm going to be looking for a job soon as well. I should be coming to get my things today."

"Well I won't be here." She snapped.

"Ok well I'll let myself in and leave my key on the kitchen table"

"You're leaving you're key! Look Mia, I'll treat you better, I promise. I won't just cast you aside or whatever you said, I'll listen when you have something to say. Please, do you know how much this new assistant is costing me?"

"Goodbye Jennifer." Before she could say another word I put down the receiver.

I walked into James' bedroom and placed another log on the fire. I watched it crackle and spark then gave it a poke with the brass fork that was leaning against the stone. It had a carved lion sitting on the top wearing a crown and was surprisingly heavy.

I walked across the room and opened the French doors and stepped out onto the cold, frosted balcony.

The man on the radio had said that the snow would only last a few days, it had been a week and the snow was as thick as ever. The wind blew and made me shiver. I turned around to go back into the warmth but was confronted by James.

"Morning." He said wrapping his arms round me.

"I hope I didn't wake you."

"No. Come on inside it's cold." He led me back in and kissed me. "I'm going to work today. I've got ten clients that I've been neglecting, so I'll be out most of today." I felt sad. James had taken a well-deserved week off and we'd spent most of it in bed. It was a shame it had to end.

"What are you going to do?"

"If it's alright with you could I get some things from the apartment and bring them back here, like clothes and some sentimental things?"

"Of course you can, can't spend you're life living in my T-shirts. I put your clothes you do have here, in the top draw in the guest bedroom."

"Which one is that?" His house was big and had many rooms. It had been passed down his family over four generations. He's never lived anywhere else. All I knew was that his parents were both Lawyer's and were very well off. He was an only child so James got everything. I assumed, as they weren't here, that they had died. But I dare not ask. James didn't seem to want to talk about them.

"Remember we made love in the really big fireplace?"

"Oh yes." I giggled and bit my bottom lip mischievously. "I remember."

The fireplace in that room was so big you could stand up in it. It hadn't been used since James used to have friends round as a boy and his housekeeper still insists on cleaning it.

I walked down the stairs to the kitchen and opened the cupboard door to get some bread. There was non in there. We had only stepped out of the house to walk penny round the garden so James hadn't been shopping. He'd also given Lillian, his housekeeper, the week off so the place was filthy. Her name is spelled Lillian, James had said But you pronounce it *Lilly-Ann* as I kept saying it wrong.

"You want me to do some cleaning today?" I asked as he stepped into the kitchen.

"No, don't be silly. I pay Lillian to do that, she'll be back today." He looked through the cupboards. "There's nothing to eat is there."

"I'll find something. You get showered and ready for work." I looked in the fridge. There was a box of eggs a little bit of milk some cheese and one slice of bacon. I got them all out and turned on the hob. I looked through the lower cupboards and found some potatoes. I boiled the potatoes and chopped them up. I then fried the eggs, milk, cheese and bacon together with the potatoes and presented James with an omelet when he came back from the shower.

"Ooo, I could get used to this, thank you!" He said gratefully wolfing down his breakfast. "I was lonely in the shower without you. Though I did have more room to actually wash not just... you know." He winked at me.

"I know." I said and smiled coyly.

Lillian came bursting into the Kitchen carrying some bags of shopping. She was covered in snow and looking very wind swept. Her little red nose shone like a beacon.

"Hey kids." She said joyfully. I'd met her a few days ago when she'd caught James and I in the conservatory. She was a lot nicer than Marie.

"You thinking of going to work today then are ya?" She said looking at James. "Well good luck, it's blowing a gale out there."

"It is? That must have come on very quickly, it was so still this morning when we got up wasn't it!"
They both looked at me for my opinion, so I nodded. "Yes, I was out on the balcony this morning, there was a slight breeze but nothing to indicate a gale."

"Well if ya don' believe me look for ya selves."
We both looked over to the kitchen window that over looked the back garden. The snow must have deepened another inch in the last hour.

"Wow." James said. "Well I gave my word so I have to go in today. I'll be all right."

"You working at the hospital?" Lillian asked.

"No the Care Center."

"Well that's not so bad, it's within walking distance." He then looked at me. "You still going to get your things?"

"Yes if I can find my way back."

"It's quite easy. You know that alley my balcony overlooks?" He waited for me to nod, then continued. "Well, go down there and you'll be in your street. It's a lot quicker than going through the park, it'll only take you five minutes. You wouldn't have noticed at the time but one of the bedrooms overlooks your apartment." He winked at me again and grabbed his coat that was hanging in the hallway.

"What, are you two animals?!" Lillian declared, pretending to be disgusted.

"I'll see you later." He moved in towards me and kissed me.

"Have a lovely day." I said and kissed him again.

He lifted the latch and stepped out. The hall was suddenly filled with the cold from outside, the snow was falling horizontally and James' shoulders were covered in a few seconds.

"I'll be back about five." He kissed me again and headed towards the Park.

I stood at the door and watched him walk away.

"I know it pains you to see him leave but you're not going to last in this world for very long if you catch pneumonia."

She pulled me in and pushed against the strong wind to shut the door. It clicked shut but I could still feel the cold coming in through the cracks. Lillian pulled the curtains across the door as if reading my mind.

"You eaten yet lovely?"

"No. James had the last of the contents of the fridge and cupboards."

"Well not anymore, there's loads in there now. What you want?" She asked walking back into the kitchen.

"Oh I'll make myself something."

"Don't be silly, I've only been looking after myself this week and it's been frightfully dull, please let me make ya breakfast or I'll just go mad!"

"Ok." I laughed. "I'd murder some eggy bread."

"Ooo good choice, I'll have some too." She looked me up and down. "Why don't you go and get dressed. I'll call you when it's ready." I thanked her and ran upstairs, the stone floor in the kitchen was biting and I was grateful to be walking on carpet again.

I went into the room I thought was the room where my clothes were but it was what looked like a study. It looked very clean, but unused. Displayed across the walls were pictures of fighter planes. There were two desks one under each window. On one desk was a picture of a pretty lady and on the other was a picture of a man who looked very much like James. There were files still piled up on the two desks one of them read, 'Peter Mathews verses the crown.' I then looked over to the other desk at the pile of folders and that read 'The crown verses

Peter Mathews.' They must have been against each other in the case. That's rare, I thought. Well at least I think it is anyway. Seemed to me very strange that a married couple would be going against each other in court and it not being a divorce. There was a coffee mug on one and a teacup on the other. Then something in the corner of the room caught my eye, the waste paper basket was rocking side to side. I stood and watched it in amazement. It then got faster and faster until suddenly it tipped up, spilling its contents on to the floor. My hair stood up on end at the back of my neck then with out me touching it the coffee cup tipped over. I gasped and spun round to see what had made the noise. I then heard footsteps outside the door, I quickly picked up the coffee cup and ran over to pick up the scrunched up bits of paper that had fallen from the waist paper basket.

"It's sad ain't it!"

I gasped in fright and jumped to my feet. "What is?"

"He not told you yet?" Lillian ran a yellow duster across the pictures and wiped inside the coffee mug and the teacup.

I carried on picking up the papers. "Told me what?"

"About his parents."

"No, I only know they were lawyers."

I watched her wipe the desk and then under the files, but she did it so carefully so as not to upset anything.

"They were murdered."

I looked at her shocked. My knees felt weak. I leaned against the nearest desk for support. "What?"

"When James was ten they were doing this case." She pointed to the files. "The first case they had ever done where they were against each other. Anyway Lydia, James' mum, was working against Peter Mathews, who was being tried for rape and murder. She had an anonymous phone call one night saying that someone had enough evidence for the case that it would surely nail the bastard. She was so excited. I can remember her running down the stairs to tell Richard, James' Father, the news. Richard said that she couldn't go, it was late and that she should wait till tomorrow. She didn't know the person and she could be putting herself in danger. But Lydia was insistent on going and went anyway. About two minutes later Richard went out after her. The phone was ringing, but he ignored it and left. I picked it up, it was the police informing us that Peter Mathews had escaped from where he was being held and that, we should stay at home, with all doors and windows locked, as we could be in danger. I ran out after Richard but I couldn't see him anywhere. It was the last time we saw them alive. They were found dead the next day, round the back of where they worked. Lydia had been hung and Richard was found shot dead at her feet. I couldn't stand to let James be adopted, so I decided to look after him myself." A small tear rolled down Lillian's cheek and she quickly wiped it away. "James insists on this room being kept exactly as it was when they were last in here. He allows me to dust it but that's it."

I stood there stunned. You only think things like that happen in films never to actual people.

"Poor James." I said, trying to imagine what it must have been like to lose both you're parents, on the same night. Lillian walked over and rubbed my arm.

"Come on." She said, "Our breakfast is getting cold." She led me out of the room. "You quickly get dressed." She said pointing to the next room. "You're clothes are in there. I'll go and put the kettle on."

I slowly turned the handle and poked my head round the door.

"Oh I remember." I said out loud. Recognizing the fireplace. The room was freezing. I opened the top draw of the chest of draws. My clothes had been washed and ironed. I took off the shirt and James boxers that I was wearing and got dressed. My clothes were cold too and I shivered as I pulled up my trousers.

I looked around the room. There was an old toy chest in the corner. Curiosity got the better of me and so I walked over and tried the lid. It was very heavy but I managed to lift it and gently rest it on the wall behind. There was a thick blanket over the top, I lifted it out gently and placed it on the bed. I looked into the chest, it was filled with little jumpers and dresses and baby grows, Tiny little skirts and baby shoes. These couldn't have been James', all the clothes were mostly pink. Then a horrible thought dawned on, something which Lillian had not mentioned. Lydia was pregnant. I knelt down beside the chest, how could the world be so cruel. How is it that people should be allowed to live in the world and be so evil? Lydia must have known that she was having a girl. I wondered if James knew, he must have done.

I stood up and went to put the blanket back when something caught my eye. It was an unfinished embroidered door hanging, with very fine needlework. It read '*Molly Youn*' that must have been the unborn babies name. My heart was filled with sadness. This house was full of secrets. It was so old it must be harboring a few. I put the blanket back and reluctantly, I closed the chest. I felt like I was shutting in a life that was never lived.

Chapter Ten

After I had left Doctor Grey's room I went back up to the recovery ward. The impatient nurse from before was sitting on my bed.

"You can go back upstairs now. The Doctor rang up and said to escort you back."

"Ok, I said, I'll get my things."

"You don't have any things." I looked at her. She had her hands on her hips and was looking towards the door. I think she was chewing on some gum, as her mouth was going a mile a minute. How did she get this job? I thought to myself. The impatience and incompetence made me feel angry.

"I don't think you're allowed to chew gum!" I said nastily and walked out leaving her standing there. She quickly scurried up behind me and tried to keep up. "Could you bloody slow down!"
I quickly turned around to look at her face to face.

"I'm sorry, was I being impatient! Maybe it was because I couldn't be bothered to wait for you, or maybe it could be because I have a man waiting for a shag in a cupboard somewhere! You know I don't know how you got this job, but believe me, if I ever see you treat a patient with the same disrespect as you treated me, I will have you fired!"

The nurse gulped.

"Nurse Johnson." I said flicking her name tag with my finger. She walked with me to my room. I opened the door with ease, They must have fixed it. I turned to look back at her as she stood in the doorway. "What are you doing, waiting for a tip? I'm here, you can go now." She walked out and I kicked my door closed with my foot.

"Argh." I screamed out loud and threw the freshly pressed towels off my bed and onto the floor. "I feel so stupid!" I heard a knock at the door and I flung it open.

"What!" I said through clenched teeth. It was Doctor Grey. My breath caught in my throat.

"I need to discuses something with you." He said looking around to see who was watching and stepped into my room and closed the door.

"I'm really..." I started, but before I finished he had swept me up into his arms and kissed me. I was shocked to begin with but then kissed him back. His arms moved from my neck and slowly down to the small of my back. Then with one hand, he moved back up my body, to hold me under my jaw and the other one pressed me tighter against him. He slowly pulled away and ran his tongue over his lips.

"I better go." He said sadly, "I don't want to, but I must."

"Ok." I whispered, in slight shock "Bye."

He twisted the handle on my bedroom door, I stepped forward to hold the door for him and he gently kissed me again. He stepped out of my room and said loudly. "Well I'm glad your door has been fixed and we will find out about you're journal and let you know of anything we find out." He slyly winked at me and headed back to his office. A twinge of excitement leaped up through my stomach and tingled in my chest. Wow! I thought. I turned and went back into my room.

I read through my journal, every page was there. Lights out was hours ago, but the nurse on duty made an exception for me so I could read. I had run myself a bath but it must have gotten cold by now. I put my hand in and I felt the cool water rise up my arm. I pulled the plug out and wiped my arm on my towel, that was still sprawled across my bedroom floor. I climbed in to bed just as the nurse came in.

"I think you should turn…"

"I was just going to." I said with a smile. "Thank you for letting me stay up." The nurse smiled and stepped in and sat down on my bed.

"I want to apologize for what happened last night. It was really unfair but it had to be done." I looked down at my blanket and ran the soft cotton between my fingers and thumb.

"I like you," she continued, "Compared to how you were and how you are now. You're a lot nicer and easier to look after, than all those other girls."

"Do you really have to look after me?"

"No that's what I'm saying. You know you're the only girl here who strips her own bed on washing days and divides your washing into light and dark colours."

"I am!" I exclaimed. "I assumed that, that was the standard thing to do. We're not in a hotel."

"See, you're so nice, and that's why I felt so guilty when we had to drug you."

I lent forward and touched her hand.

"It's in the passed."

"Thank you. You know I was on duty that day Doctor Grey took you're journal to be photocopied."

"Oh?"

"Yes, he asked me to cover for him. So whilst he was photocopying I stood in the doorway pretending to mop. Then the governor came passed, I thought we were busted, but then I had the idea of pretending to be in the process of cleaning the room, so he couldn't go in there. You see he's very hung up on patient's privacy and if he found out what Doctor Grey was doing, without you're consent, he'd get very cross."

"Wow I didn't know that."

"Yes, and then he had to be quick to get it back to you so you didn't know he'd taken it. He was so worried if you ever found out what he'd done, you'd hate him. You don't hate him do you Hilary?"

"No, no I don't hate him. In fact, after what happened to my original, I'd be lost if it wasn't for him making a copy, no I don't hate him, I lo…" I stopped short before continuing to proclaim my love for a Doctor to a nurse.

"I like him even more for doing so."

"Oh good. You know he thinks the world of you. Out of all his patients you're the one that's come the furthest in the time you've been here." She smiled. "You've got a good friend there Hilary, look after him." I felt my heart fill with love for the man. I wanted to run and hold him in my arms and never let go. "I'd better go and let you get some rest. Maybe we can talk again tomorrow night, would that be ok?"

"Of course." I said, now happy, that I'd finally found a friend. "Oh I'm sorry I don't know your name."

"Sarah." She replied and gently closed the door behind her. She pulled it shut hard until I heard the click, I then heard her feet walking away back to her desk.

* * *

I sat in the communal room writing in my journal when Wart girl Chloe walked in and sat down on the sofa immediately opposite. She had her legs spread wide open and her hands cradling the back of her, head. She was wearing baggy jeans and a rugby shirt. Her hair was done up into a tight bun and she had no make up on. I looked up at her so she knew I knew, she was there. She sucked in her teeth and stood up. She looked around. No one was about, it was such a lovely day that they were all in the garden. Chloe came over and sat next to me. I had my feet up on the sofa and quickly turned and put them on the floor, she'd snap my ankles if she sat on them.

"I heard you got a little present when you were down in the hospital ward."

I stopped writing and looked up at her. "How do you know about that?" As if I have to ask, I thought.

"Oh a little bird told me." She lent in and beckoned for me to move closer. I reluctantly moved my head, so her mouth was a few inches from my ear. "You should really watch who you talk to. Doctor Grey told us everything." I felt my chest go tight and my body tense. "He told us everything, how you screamed out and started crying. He said you were a right old baby, crying like that over a stupid journal."

I turned my head and looked her right in the eyes. "You are a Bitch!" I whispered softly and turned back to my writing.

After dinner I sat in my room and I heard shouting. I opened the door to find Doctor Grey, Governor Jones and the nasty Nurse from the hospital ward arguing in the hallway.

"I did not!" She kept saying. Slowly all the girls popped their head out of their bedrooms to see what all the fuss was about.

"You are through as a nurse!" The Governor yelled. The nurse looked up at him and ran out of the double doors. Doctor Grey looked up and saw me. He touched the Governors arm and motioned that he was coming over.

"What's happened?" I asked

"We were told by one of the girls that Nurse Johnson had something to do with you're journal going missing."

"Really!"

"Yes, she had the key to your room and broke in, whilst you were in the bath."

"But my door wasn't shut properly. You wouldn't need a key."

"Well that may be so, but she's not entitled to a key, she just works on the hospital ward down stairs, she had no need to be up here, so she must have stolen it."

Then Governor Jones walked over and said. "We do not tolerate invasion of privacy in this hospital or stealing." He had a very deep voice. He looked at my photocopied journal in my hand. "Nice to see you made a copy. Who did that for you?"

I stopped and thought, I didn't want Doctor Grey to get into trouble, but I didn't really want to get into trouble either.

"A few days ago, I asked Doctor Grey to give me his word not to read it, but could he please make a copy for me, he agreed."

Doctor Grey smiled slightly.

"And you didn't read it Doctor?"

"Of course not, I gave my word."

"Well keep me informed on anything more you hear."

"I will, thank you."

He nodded and walked away.

"Would you like to come in?" I whispered.

"I shouldn't." He said. "I want to, but I really shouldn't."

He turned to walk away.

"Hold on." I called out.

He turned back to look at me.

"Wart girl, I mean Chloe said that you told everyone about what happened in the hospital ward. She said that you were saying what a baby I was crying over a stupid journal."

He stared at me dumbstruck. "Please tell me you don't believe her."

"Oh god, of course I don't!" I looked at his hurt expression. "No Doctor I didn't believe her for a moment."

"Good, it was that nurse who told everyone. And it was Chloe who came to us and told us what had happened."

"Really? But, what I'm confused about is why that nurse would want to take my Journal. I had never met her before until I woke up in the hospital ward, yes she was very rude to me, but I don't think she stole and burnt my journal."

Doctor Grey studied my face and his forehead wrinkled to a frown. "You really don't think she did it?"

"No I really don't think she did. I think she probably told everyone what a 'baby' I was, but I don't think she stole anything."

"Well do you still think its Wart girl, I mean Chloe?" He corrected himself.

"Yes I do, she's the only one who has any reason to."

Doctor Grey sighed. "I don't think there's anyway we can prove that."

"Yes there is, I'll just have to make her confess to me with you in ear shot." I lowered my voice even more to a very soft whisper. "Ok, when everyone is in the garden tomorrow I'll be in the communal room and she'll come and talk to me. I'll get her to confess."

He looked doubtful but agreed.

"I'll see you later for our meeting."

I smiled excitedly.

"Oh, and I thought I asked you to call me Robert."

"Too personal." I replied sadly.

He nodded reluctantly and walked away.

"Bye Doctor Grey." I heard Julie call out.

Before I closed my door, I saw Chloe walk passed. She looked over at me and smirked.

"Shame ain't it." She said referring towards the nurse. "I'm just on my way for my meeting with Doctor Grey." She wet her lips and tried to wiggle her fat hips as she entered his office. Before she went in, she turned and gave me a wave. She looked in at him "Yum." She mouthed and closed the door.

She makes me so angry! I think I actually really hate her. I knew it was her, who took my journal and then she told the Governor it was the nurse, so she wouldn't be found out. I hate what happened to my journal, but I don't want to see someone suffer for something they didn't do. Even if it was that horrible nurse.

Chapter eleven

A few days later, James and I were sitting on a bench in Hyde Park finishing spring rolls that we had bought from the Chinese take away, just across the way. James had finished work for the day and the afternoon stretched out before us. We were watching people doing Christmas shopping. I usually spent Christmas with Jennifer, but she hadn't invited me yet, so I assumed I wasn't wanted. James sat silently picking bean sprouts out of his teeth.

"Everything ok?"

"Yep." He answered abruptly.

I said no more. I knew by now that if I wanted James to talk to me, the best way to go about it was to show complete lack of interest. Sure enough, he pulled something out of his jacket pocket.

"What's this?" I asked as he handed me an opened envelope.

"Just read it and tell me what you think."

I carefully slid the note out and unfolded the paper. It was a letter written on pretty flowery paper and the handwriting was beautiful. It read.

To our beloved James, hope all is well. What are you doing over Christmas? We are in town and are hoping that we can run into you. Mikie's doing well and we're sure you would like to meet him. We will be at Penelope's Tea Room this Saturday at 2.00pm if you care to join us. Yours friends Claire, Kristine and Michael.

"Well it's Saturday today and it's one o clock now." I said looking at my watch, "Who are they?" I asked, folding the letter and putting it back in its envelope.

"Well Claire is my ex-girlfriend and Kristine is her lover or 'life partner' as they all liked to be called."
I could detect a hint of anxiety in his voice.

"Have you not seen them then since..."

"Yes." He interrupted, "It's just that. Would you come with me?"

"Of course I will, there's nothing weird about going for Tea, with my boyfriend's ex-girlfriend and her lover."

"If you don't want to come, that's fine."

"No, I'll come with you, it's fine." I handed him back the letter and he put it back in his pocket.

"So I'm your boyfriend, am I?"
I felt embarrassed. I could feel the blood rise to my cheeks. Oh don't put me on the spot like that.
He laughed and put his arm over my shoulder. "Don't worry, I've been telling everyone at work what a wonderful new girlfriend I have." He lent over and kissed my forehead, "And how beautiful you are."
I bent my head upwards and kissed him. I felt my embarrassment being replaced with tenderness. "Ooh your nose is cold." I said pulling away as his nose touched my cheek.

"So's yours." He said and rubbed his nose against mine.
I looked down at my watch. It read 1:15, where's Penelope's Tea Room?"

"Oh not that far. Are you getting cold sitting here? I am." He said as he lit a cigarette. He stood up and took my gloved hand.
Jennifer never gave me my gloves back, so James bought me a new

pair. "Let's go."

We walked through the Park with the snow crunching under our feet. It hadn't snowed for days now, but it was still cold enough for it to still be deep on the ground. Every now and then there was a patch, where you could see little blades of grass poking out above the snow. There had been hundreds of power cuts over the week, because of the bad weather, so all the schools had been closed since Tuesday. The kids were loving it.

James said something that snapped me out of my day Dream.

"Sorry James, what did you say?"

"I said I bet the kids have loved having the whole of this week off, and now there's no school till after Christmas."

"That's what I was just thinking."

He gave my hand a squeeze. "You're gonna like Clair and Kristine."

"I'm sure I will. How old is Michael?"

James stopped and thought for a moment. "He is six months, I think." He paused then asked, "Do you get broody easily?"

I smiled at the bazaar question.

"I've never really had time to think much about babies, anyway I'm only nineteen. I'm not really ready to think about them yet. Jennifer was enough of a baby anyway."

James let out a slight laugh. "This is where you fell!" He said pointing towards a patch of snow under a big oak tree. "You must have twisted your ankle, or something, cos you fell flat on your face. Luckily I was walking penny at the time and was there to help you. I ran over to help you up, but you were out cold. There was no one else near by in the park, if I hadn't been here, you may have suffocated in the snow."

I'd never been close to death. "Thank you."

"Well I'm glad I was there to be your rescuer, who knows you might have been rescued by an incredible handsome, rich prince who whisked you away and I would had never seen you again!"

I giggled. "I can safely say that I am happy *you* found me."

He kissed my forehead and we carried on towards the entrance of the Park.

"I've never been down here before!" I exclaimed, as James led me down a narrow street that still looked lost in the eighteen hundreds.

"It's beautiful isn't it."

I looked up the cobbled street and saw a sign in the shape of a teacup on the wall. As we walked closer it read *Penelope's Tea Rooms*.

"We're here." He said and looked in through the window. "There they are." He pointed towards the two women sitting at the round table, furthest away from the door, then straightened up and looked at me. His manner had completely changed, he felt stiff and uneasy.

I took his hand in mine. "We going in then?"

"Hold on!" He said quickly turning his back to the window. "No matter what, you must promise to think no less of me, no matter what is said. Don't judge until you have spoken to me about it later." He then kissed me hard on the lips and led me into the warm Tea room. A feeling of anxiety came over me. I didn't know what he meant, by not judging him, what could possibly be said?

One of the women looked up as we approached their table. "James." She smiled and welcomed him into her embrace. "And you are?" She held out her hand for me to shake.

"Mia."

"Well any friend of James is a friend of mine, I'm Claire and this is Kristine." Claire opened stretched out her arm and beckoned Kristine to stand and shake my hand.

"Nice to meet you." She smiled. Her eyes were a bright blue and her whole face lit up when she smiled.

I nodded, "Nice to meet you."

James pulled one of the two empty chairs out and let me sit down. Then he sat beside me and rested his hand on my leg, I think more for his comfort than mine.

"So Claire, Kristine how you been?"

"We're getting married!" They both said at the same time.

Everyone in the tea room stopped their conversations and look around at our table.

"Wow." James said, clearly not knowing what to say.

"Don't be surprised James, you've always known how much I've wanted to get married and now the government have made it legal, we're wasting no time." Claire said lifting up Kristine's hand, so we could both see the rings. They weren't anything glamorous, but they were pretty.

"We're going to have a Pagan wedding, and then we'll go to the registry office after."

"Where you going to be married?"

"Glastonbury." They both said.

"I thought as much." James said nodding.

There was an uncomfortable moment of silence.

"So who's this little one then?" I said leaning over to the pram.

"Oh this is Mikie." Claire said reaching in and pulling out a big blob dressed in babies clothing. "He's getting heavy."

I felt James freeze as he saw the baby. "What do you think James?"

"He's beautiful." He said swallowing hard.

"Would you like to hold him?" Kristine asked.

James shook his head. "No thank you."

"So who's mummy?" I asked looking at the two women cuing over him.

"I am." Kristine said.

"Oh I think the little fellers hungry." Claire said passing the 'little' feller to Kristine.

She took him and stood up. "Don't hold your breath, once he gets going there's no stopping him."

I can imagine. I felt like saying. But I didn't, I just smiled "See you in a minute."

* * *

93

We sat in Penelope's Tea Room for over an hour, James and Claire swapping stories about the times they shared together and Kristine spending most of it in the mother and baby room.

"So you two together?" Claire asked looking at me.

"Yes we are." I answered reaching out for his hand, he gently placed it in mine and gave it a squeeze.

"Two weeks."

"Only two?" She looked surprised. "Well, that's good James 'cos you haven't dated anyone since you and me." She looked at me, "And that was two years ago."

I looked up at James fondly.

"So, if you don't mind me saying, how old are you?"

"I'm nineteen."

"Nineteen? Well, what's age nowadays, anyway hu?" Her voice changed its tone slightly. I think she could see I was puzzled. "James is twenty nine. Don't tell me you didn't know."

James stiffened again and Claire looked like she'd just gained a point in whatever game we were playing. She sat back looking pleased with herself.

I looked at James. He had clenched his jaw tight. Anyone would have thought she was jealous. James and I hadn't discussed our ages. It didn't seem to matter. Today in the park, was the first time I had mentioned how old I was and he didn't say anything. Either he didn't hear or he didn't mind.

James slowly dropped his head and picked at an invisible thread on his trousers.

Jennifer would kill me, if she found out how old he was, ten years was quite a lot. Anyway, he would have known how old I was because of the papers.

Thankfully Kristine came back with Mikie for the second time and sat with us. She looked around. "Everyone ok?"

"Yes, just fine." Said Claire with a victory look on her face.

Nothing else was said on the matter and Kristine asked me what I did,

I explained about Jennifer. She had heard of her and was very impressed to meet 'The Bathroom Baby'.

"So you're nice and young then." She said, "Not like us old pensioners." She laughed kindly.

"She's nineteen." Said Claire spitefully.

"Yes I worked that out, thank you darling. Here." She said, passing Mikie over to her.

"I like your coat." I said pointing to the green coat, draped over her chair.

"It's lovely isn't it? A friend of mine used to make clothes for Gucci Armani and she made this for me. Anyone got a pen and paper?" She looked at James and Claire, who were both sat in silence. They shook their heads.

"Oh actually, yes I do." He fished in his coat pocket and pulled out Claire's letter. "Write on that."

All three of us looked at Claire who had sat up sharply in her seat, with a look of shock on her face.

Kristine shrugged and wrote down a name and address. "She lives near here, just tell her Kristine Richions sent you and she'll do you a really good deal."

"Thank you." I said taking the letter and handing it back to James.

"No you keep it, I'll only loose it." He said looking over at Claire, who glared back at him. "Well we'd better be on our way. It was nice to see you Kristine." He said leaning over and kissing her cheek, "Look after that baby of yours."

"Our baby!" Exclaimed Claire, jumping to her feet and putting her arm around Kristine.

"Bye little man." I said giving Michael a little wave.

He gurgled in response and kicked out his leg.

"Bye Claire." James said taking my hand and literally pulling me out of the Teashop.

He stopped just outside the door. "I'm sorry I."

I didn't let him finish. I pulled his head down and kissed him. I didn't care how old he was, he might be twenty-nine years old, but he was my twenty nine year old and that was all that mattered.

"So it doesn't bother you?"

"We never discussed our age and even if we did I'd still be here."

"So would I." He kissed me again and took my hand.

I looked back through theTeashop's window, as we walked away and saw Kristine sorting out Mikie in his pram and Claire staring at, bemused.

"If she's so jealous, why did she leave you?" I asked as we walked through the park.

"It's the old, she doesn't want me, but she doesn't want anyone else to have me, thing."

"That's a bit childish, and the baby, is he registered as both of theirs, or is he just Kristine's?"

"I was afraid that question would be asked, I'm surprised Claire didn't use it as a weapon to attack us with. They wanted to have a baby, well Kristine definitely did, so I said that as long as Kristine was the one having the baby, I would donate my, you know."

"Donate?"

"Yes she used my, you know, inside her, you know."

"Yeah I know."

He stopped and held me by both shoulders. "I have nothing to do with him, he is Claire's and Kristine's baby. I merely gave them the ingredient's they needed. Otherwise it would have cost them thousands."

"Is that why you didn't hold him at Tea?"

He nodded. "Are you ok about all that?"

"So he won't come knocking on your door in eighteen years time to find his birth father."

"No, the only way I'd get him is if they both died. They've put me down as next of kin in their Wills."

"Ok," I said. "I can live with that."

He kissed me and we carried on walking home. You had to hand it to him, that was a generous thing to do, considering the circumstances. I wasn't entirely sure about how I felt about it though. I just kept thinking, if James and I get really serious, I could be almost like a stepmother, before we've even started.

Chapter twelve

Just as the weatherman had promised the next day was beautiful. I was already up and dressed by nine. It was now ten-thirty and all the nurses were rushing around, trying to get everyone up, so we could spend the day in the garden.

Kate was sitting on the windowsill as usual. "I can't find my hat." She shrieked.

"Well are you looking for it?" Came one of the nurses' replies.

"No."

"Well go and look for it then and you might find it."

Julie came out of her bedroom, wearing an Indians outfit, I think she was meant to be Pocahontas. She had her hair in plates and what I could only guess was lipstick as war paint.

I walked over to the window and looked out. "You seen him yet today?"

"No," She said sadly. "I'm beginning to think that he's not around this time of year."

"Oh really?" I said generally sounding surprised, slight break through there. "So you going to stop looking for him, until we're closer to Christmas?"

"Oh no," She said, "I'd hate for him to come by and I not see him." Maybe not. "Would you like me to help you find your hat?"

She grinned and nodded her head.

I took her hand and led her to her room. She had her eyes fixed on the window, till the last second, when we walked into her bedroom. I'd never been in there before, the room was pink, like mine, but she had little fair figures stuck on the wall. She had fairy bedding and headboard. Her room was a lot more homely than mine. She had teddies and dolls, lots of pictures and cards from friends and family.

I felt sad, that she had such a lovely room and all these people writing to her, saying how much they loved her, yet she was in here.

I also felt sad, because my room was nothing like this, not because I wanted fairy bedding, but I had no cards from loved ones, only one picture of my mother on a shelf. I had such a fantastic life outside of this hospital, but I had nothing but my memories in my journal to show for it. Where had my life gone?

"Ok, you look in that chest of drawers and I'll look in your wardrobe. Ok?"

Kate nodded and started looking. "First one to find it is the winner!"

I started looking quicker, so she knew she had competition. I lifted up an old jumper at the top of her cupboard and her hat fell down along with something else and landed on the floor. I bent down and picked up the mystery item. It was a photograph, it was signed and dated onthe back. It read in scruffy handwriting *Christopher and Kathryn Marks 1988* that was the year Kate was born. I turned the photograph over to see the front. It was a dull colored picture of a nice looking man, kissing a newborn baby. He looked so happy and full of love for his little bundle.

"No!" Kate snatched the photograph out of my hand and put it in her pocket.

"Who?" But her uneasiness made me stop my questioning.

She shuffled her feet and bit her bottom lip. "My daddy was the man and I was the baby. It was the only time he had his picture taken with me. It's the only one I have. Please don't take it away from me." She began to sound frantic.

"Take it away, why would I do that?"

"Cos you're a grown up and that's what grown ups do, they take special things away."

She looked so sad and hurt. I wanted to hold her and tell her that everything was going to be ok, but I didn't know that. I didn't know if everything was going to be ok. "Would you like a hug?"

She stepped towards me and let me embrace her. Even though she was seventeen years of age, I wanted to mummy her, look after her and keep her safe.

She sniffed and buried her face into my shoulder. "You smell like my mummy." She said rubbing her face into my jumper.

"Is that a good thing?"

"Of course, my mummy is an angel."

"I'm sure she'd love to hear you say that."

"She can't, she died when I was five, she had a heart attack."

"Oh I am sorry Kate, that must have been horrible." She didn't say anything, she just stood, quietly and held on to me.

There was a little tap and Doctor Grey popped his head round the door. "Ready girls? They're waiting for you."

"Oh I found your hat."

Kate broke away and I picked up the little pink hat off the floor and handed it to her.

She gave me a half smile and walked out of her room to join the others.

Doctor Grey stepped in, "What was that all about?"

"Nothing." I lied, shaking my head. "She just needed a bit of looking after and someone to talk to."

"That's not your job, Hilary."

I felt cross at that remark, are patients not allowed to hug each other anymore! "Well you people stick us in a hospital all together, what else are we supposed to do, apart from help heal each other?"

"Worry about healing yourselves for starters."

"Maybe that's what we are doing. By being friends with others and helping them through their time of hardship, we'll help ourselves to realize who we are."

"But anything she discuses should be with me, so I know and I can help."

"Do you really think that that's the only way! Oh don't be so short sighted Doctor you're not god!"

I quickly walked passed him to get away, but he grabbed my hand and pulled me back.

"You're right." He said "Maybe you guys do help each other, but do you really think you are helping her, if you keep what she said from me?"

"Yes I do, because this particular thing, there is nothing you can do."

"Try me."

I looked up at him into his wide pleading eyes. As a man I would trust him with my life, as a Doctor I wouldn't. He'd take that photograph away and poor Kate would have nothing. Even though her father abused her, he was still her father and she obviously needs that picture, as it's the only thing of love that connects him to her. "I'm sorry Doctor, you guys are all up there with the privacy thing, well so am I. "

I felt him soften, "Well at least you're loyal. I admire that." He looked around and kissed my forehead. "You ready to get Wart girl? She lost the privilege of going outside today, because she started another fight with one of the girls at breakfast."

"I'm ready." I shuddered with nervous and excitement.

He nodded and walked to his office. He opened the window, that opened out into the communal room.

His office was built in the oldest part of the hospital and then a few hundred years later they added our part, why the window was still there we'll never know.

I looked over at the sofas, Chloe was sitting with her stupid thumb in her mouth, taking up half the sofa and had a look on her face that would kill on sight.

"Why you not outside with the others?" I asked as I approached her.

"They said I'm not allowed out today."

"Why not?"

"Because I had a fight with one of the girls at breakfast. I'm not a morning person that's all and that girl is always so cheerful."

"Sally?" I asked

"Yeah." Chloe sat up and looked at me. "Do you find that too? She's always so *over* happy, that's the trouble. Even after a session with Doctor Grey she's all *'ooh that was just wonderfully refreshing.'*
She imitated Sally to a tee and made me giggle. "She is quite a lot to handle sometimes. What was the fight over?"

"She said what a lovely morning it was and I told her she could put that morning, where the sun doesn't shine, if you pardon the pun."

"What did she do?" I was actually quite intrigued.

"She threw her tray at me and said that I'd be a lot prettier, if I smiled. I mean what sought of come back is that!" Chloe started to laugh. Sally was right, she was a lot prettier when she smiled.

"But then she started to throw everyone else's tray at me and the nurses had to grabbed her and take her to her room."

"You get hurt?"

"A little." She rolled up her top and showed me her ribs. They were slightly bruised, but not anything serious.

"Are you all right?"

"Yeah I'm ok, so she's locked in her room and they've banned me from going out today. I just did what everyone was wishing they had the guts to do."

"You're very good at speaking your mind. I've had a piece of it myself."

"I get fired up very quickly. I am sorry I called you an old trout, you are quite pretty for your age."

I paused, not quite sure what to make of what she had said.

"I do like you. You've had a very interesting life." She hesitated and stared at me panic stricken. "I, I." She stuttered

"You read my journal!"

"Not all of it. You should make it into a book, it is very interesting." She spoke fast.

"Then why did you burn it?" I could feel my anger rise up in my throat.

"Because I was mad at you for calling me fat and ugly and smelly."

I heard a noise in the door way to the communal room and as planned Doctor Grey stepped in. "I heard that Chloe. How dare you do such a thing!"

Chloe wrenched herself up out of her seat. She looked like a rabbit caught in headlights. "I'm sorry, I was just so angry at you."

"So you decided to destroy my only possession, the only thing I have that connects me to out there!" I motioned towards the door.

"I am so sorry."

"Come on you've got to come with me." Said Doctor Grey.

Chloe let him lead her towards the door. "No, please you have no idea how long I fought to get into this ward. The Governor will move me back down there, I'm sure. Please!"

"Hold on." I said stopping Doctor Grey from leaving. "Move you back, where?"

"Down stairs! Seriously, it is horrible down there. You have no freedom. I wasn't even aloud to pee on my own. You can't make any friends, cos they're all like zombies from the drugs we're given. I worked really hard so I could be moved up to this ward. Please don't tell him. If he finds out I can't control my anger again he'll send me back!"

I looked at her pained expression. The fear in her eyes. I then looked at Doctor Grey and he looked at me puzzled. "What are you thinking?" He asked me softly.

Without answering, I turned my attention back to Chloe, "If you promise to never loose your temper again, and think about what you say, before you speak and remember that everyone is untitled to their own opinion, not just you." I stopped and took in a deep breath. "Then maybe we won't tell the Governor."

She looked at me surprised. "Really, you would do that?"

"Really, you would?" Asked Doctor Grey confused.

"As long as you promise to look after everyone here, as if they were your own family. Yes you can stand up for yourself, but don't start the fights."

Doctor Grey looked at me perplexed. "You want me to let her go and just forget about all this!?"

I gently rested my hand on the arm that had hold of her. "She's apologized and if she keeps her promise, then I won't say another word about it," I looked back at her. "But if you don't and if Doctor Grey hears the slightest complaint about you, he will march you up to the Governors office, so fast, your head will spin."

Doctor Grey stepped aside and Chloe flung herself at me.

"Oh thank you!" She sighed with relief, throwing her arms around my neck. "No one has ever been that kind to me before. All the girls were saying how nice you are, but I chose not to believe them. Thank you so much for understanding how much I need to be up here!"

"But what about that nurse?" Doctor Grey asked Chloe. "Miss Johnson. Did she have any part to play?"

Chloe told us how the nurse *had* met me before, of which, I don't remember, and decided she didn't like me. So Chloe said that she had an idea. Miss Johnson got the key for Chloe, but it was Chloe who stole and burnt my journal. The nurse didn't have anything to do with that.

"What should we do?" I looked at Doctor Grey. I think he was still trying to keep up with it all.

"I don't know. That's your decision. If you tell the Governor it wasn't the nurse, you may have to say it was Chloe."

I sat and thought.

"If it helps." He said. "She was probably going to be fired anyway. She was so incompetent."

I nodded in agreement.

"And she was really nasty, telling everyone that you were acting like a baby, down on the ward." Chloe added.

"Then why did you say Doctor Grey told everyone?"

She looked down at her dirt ridden fingernails. "I was jealous, I know of the tight relationship you two share and I've never had that."

Doctor Grey gave me a glance then looked back at Chloe. I smiled in side. No one had ever been jealous of me before, it felt good.

"Well, let's not speak of this anymore and be friends. As long as you are nice." I add quickly with a warning look in my eye.

She nodded and thanked us both.

"Can I see you in here, for a minute, please." Doctor Grey took my hand and led me into his office.

Chloe slumped back down on the sofa and flicked the television on.

"Are you sure about this? She really hurt you." He said, clicking the door shut behind him.

"Yes, but she's also been really hurt, she just needs help with directing her anger at something other than people."

He looked up to the ceiling and closed his eyes. "That's it, I couldn't figure out what to do with that girl, we've tried nearly everything, apart from anger evasion."

"Are you being sarcastic!"

"Yes." He laughed and gave me a big hug. "You're really getting threw this." He lent over to the window and closed the blinds.

I bit my lip anxiously. "Come here." I said beckoning him to come over to me. I stood up on tiptoes and kissed him. He lifted me up and I wrapped my legs around his waist. He wasn't so fierce with his kisses, this time he was tender and gentle. I knew I couldn't have him yet, but that made my yearning for him even stronger.

Chapter thirteen

When we were on the road, I had spent a great deal of time absorbed in Magazines. My favorites, consisted of Bravo which was a Spanish magazine, and Bonjour Mode! Which is the French equivalent to England's Hello Fashion magazine. I used to love looking at all the French fashions. They wore such peculiar clothes on the Cat walk. The Magazines used to get me in such a mood, that I used to go and rummage through Jennifer's old costumes and see what bizarre outfits I could make up.

I had an old Bonjour Mode! in front of me with Jennifer on the front cover. I looked down at my mother, who I hadn't seen for over three weeks. I had gone back to the apartment to get my things, but she had had the locks changed. I banged on the door and eventually, Marie answered. She informed me that Jennifer wasn't in, but she had packed the essentials for me.

The essentials consisted of a few old magazines, two pairs of underwear a bra and a pair of jeans, and they were the patchy ones that

I had created after reading about the patchwork quilt fashion in last winters issue. If I were in Paris right now, they'd probably scold me for wearing them.

But sadly, I was not in Paris, I was back in Starbucks, in the exact same seat, I always sat in. The man from behind the counter knows my name. I think, I've heard one of the girls call him Jerry, but I dare not call him that, in case it wasn't.

The table I was sitting at, in my opinion, was the best seat in the house, I could see the people coming up the high street, going about their day to day business. But my life was different this time. I wasn't just watching other people living their lives, I was waiting for my new life to begin and right on time, in it came.

It came dressed in a Grey pencil skirt, a matching Grey suit jacket and high heels, her blonde hair was tied up in a bun and she had such an air of elegance, I could only dream of having.

She scanned the room then her eyes lit up as she saw me.

"Hello." She said sitting down. "Ooh it's bitterly cold out there!"

"I know." I was nervous. I didn't really know what else to say.

"I'm Lilly Samuels from Simply fashion and you are Mia Preston, and you are nineteen?" She read from her little notebook, she had brought out from her bag. "Is that correct?"

"Yes that is. Nice to meet you."

She smiled kindly. "Do you have any experience working for a Magazine publishers?"

"I thought the job was for a personal assistant."

"Yes it is dear, but I just need to know your history, what you've done in past jobs, etc." She said each letter separately.

"Well, I've never actually worked in a publishing company before, let alone a magazine publishing company."

"Oh?"

"But." I continued before she could say anything. "I have had a lot of dealings with the press. I can read a magazine in ten different languages, I have been a PA for the most difficult women in show business and what would your boss say, when he finds out that you've hired the Bathroom Baby?"

"You?" She said sitting back in astonishment. "You're the Bathroom Baby? Oh my god! No I don't believe you."

I moved the magazine with Jennifer on the cover towards her. "This is my mother, Jennifer Louise Preston. I've traveled round with her all my life. Doing her hair and make up, organizing her interviews and auditions. I think the whole world knows how difficult she can be, so you know that I can put up with a lot."

"Wow, so why are you no longer working with her?"

"The child's got to fly the nest some time."

"That's incredible, but this will be nothing like that, these people will treat you like something they've stepped in."

"Oh, I'm used to that. Working with Jennifer, wasn't exactly all flowers and candy."

"So if you're not working with her, are you still living with her?"

"No I've moved in with my boyfriend."

"Oh lovely, it's a shame for Jennifer though, was there a big bust up, or..?"

"A little bust up, I was taken ill for a few days and I was staying with James. I found out, she had got married, when I read that days newspaper. That was the last straw. She got married with out me and her *Maid* was her Maid of honor." God, I sounded bitter.

"So a big bust up then! So what was she like as a mother?"

"She was ok, I guess. She was always so busy with her theatre work and her social life. But I think even if she didn't have all that to tend to we would still have a strained relationship, she's just not the motherly type."

"That must have been really tough."

"Yes it was, and because we were on the move so much, it was very hard for me to make friends, so I was quite lonely."

"Oh bless you!" She sounded slightly patronizing. "Could I write an article about you?"

"Just me?"

"Just you."

"Only if I get the job." I said sternly, "Otherwise, I'm afraid no."

She started scribbled something down in her book.

I looked out of the window. The snow had started to melt and was leaving an ugly Grey slush on the ground. The sun was shinning, it was a beautiful day, but bitterly cold when the wind blew. People were on there way home from Christmas shopping. Christmas was in three weeks and I only had a little amount of money, that Jennifer had put into my bank account. I wasn't sure if she would pay me. I know she's a pain but she's not dishonest.

"Ok, could you please stand up so I can take your photo, to show the Editor."

I stood up, dusted myself off and gave a cheeky smile. Blinded for a moment, I sat back down. "Strong flash!"

She raised her shoulders and smiled. "I don't know, I'm always on this side of the camera. Ok." She started gathering her things. "Thank you for that. I will be in touch. I have some others to interview, but I *will* be in touch." She seemed pretty certain, which made me feel happy that she would.

"Well best be off, talk soon."

I stood up and shook her hand.

"Take care." I said.

I felt good about this. She seemed pretty confident, I lifted up the magazine with Jennifer on the front and slid out a Simple Fashion, that I had hid underneath. It was my favorite British magazine, it studied fashion, celebrities and really life situations, where people write in with their stories. I flicked through and found the page that was written by my new friend. It was on 'Women, proud of their wait.' It was all superficial, but living with Jennifer for the last nineteen years, was just that.

I finished reading the article and stood up to leave.

"Good bye, Mia." 'Jerry' called out from behind the coffee cups.

"Looks like it's in the bag, hu?"

"Fingers crossed." I said, lifting my crossed fingers up to my shoulder so he could see.

"Well, if it doesn't work out, you're welcome to a job here, you're in here enough, you might as well get paid for it."

I laughed. "Thank you, I'll keep that in mind. Bye." I waved, as I shut the door behind me.

A huge gust of wind blew and I had to take a few steps backwards, so as not to fall over.

I wished it would snow again, so we could all have a proper white Christmas, not a sludgy one. A thought then dawned on me. This could be my first Christmas, without Jennifer. If she keeps this 'I'm never going to see her again', pretense up that may well be the case.

*   *   *

A week had passed and I hadn't heard from Simply Fashion. I really thought I had got the job, but surely I would have heard from them by now. I explained to James what she had said, after the interview and he said it sounded pretty hopeful.

I was snuggled up in a blanket next to the fire, with Penny, after our walk in the park, when James burst in. "What's going on with the world!" He sighed as he flopped into his armchair. He lent forward and rubbed his hands together vigorously. His nails went really blue when he was cold. He blew them, trying to bring their colour back.

I got up out of my chair and walked across the living room. It wasn't a big room, considering the size of the rest of the house. But James had said that there was a bigger living room, he had blocked off, along with some other rooms, because it was too big for just him and Lillian. I knelt down in front of him and rubbed is hands. They could get really painful for him if they got too cold. He calls it Raynaud's disease.

"Feel better?"

"Yes, thank you." He tapped his thighs and I sat down on his lap. "Ok, all today my patients have been talking about your mum in this magazine." He bent down and reached into his briefcase, and pulled out a copy of simply fashion. This month, they had a free handbag, which I instantly fell in love with.

"They said to me to read this."

"Ooh, I haven't read this months yet, it only came out today, thank you." I kissed his cheek, tore away the cellophane and flicked through to see what I could learn about Jennifer this month. I stopped when I saw a picture of me, looking very disheveled in Starbucks. I read the caption out loud to James.

"Battles of the Bathroom Baby."

"Hu?" James looked over my shoulder and tried to read the article with me.

"Oh, my God. The bitch!" I jumped up off his lap and started pacing around the room. I handed the magazine to James to read. "You read it, I can't."

His eyes scanned over the two-page spread.

"Is it bad?"

James looked up at me. "Lets just hope Jennifer doesn't read this."

"Why, is it really *that* bad?"

"I had a very troubled childhood, my mother was never around so I was very much alone, in what was most of the time, a strange unknown land."

"I never said that, I said that she was busy a lot and it was hard making friends because we moved around so much, so I felt lonely."

"Did you say you were neglected?"

"No!"

"Did you say she was never the motherly type?"

"Yes, yes I said that."

"Did you say that she was so wrapped up in her own life, that she never had time for you?"

"No, that I did not say, felt like it though."

"Well, I'm afraid sweetheart, that's the same thing, why did you say anything about Jennifer anyway?"

I threw myself down on the sofa and put my hands to my head. "Oh my god, she's gonna be so mad!"

"Why did you tell them Mia?"

"Because I thought it would help me get the job." I sobbed.

James shut the magazine, stood up and walked towards me. "You know that's not the way to get a job. You get it off your own merit, not hers."

"I know that now, they never called." Just at the moment the doorbell range, I looked up at him in hope.

"No it won't be them, one, it's seven in the evening and two, do you really think they'd offer you the job after writing this about you. No, the only thing they are gonna get from you, is a letter from my Lawyer, suing their asses."

The doorbell rang again and James stepped out of the room, to go and answer it.

"Is my daughter in there?"

My breath caught in my throat.

"Jennifer!" I stumbled out of the living room and walked down the hallway.

"Look, Ms Preston I'm sure there's an explanation."

"Don't you *Ms Preston* me, this is all your fault."

"Jennifer!" I cut in. "Don't blame him, come on we'll talk outside."

I grabbed my coat and boots and pulled her by the arm, out of the door.

"How old is he anyway?"

I turned back and mouthed sorry to James, as he closed the door.

"You know I was sitting with Jimmy, having a nice dinner, in a nice restaurant, when a young girl thrust this under my nose." Jennifer said, handing me the magazine that she had rolled up into a tube.

"According to Simply Fashion, I am the worst mother, ever!" She slammed the Magazine down on the floor and dug her heal into the picture of Lindsey Lohan.

"Look Jennifer, half that stuff in there, I didn't even say."

"Well, then that just leaves us with the other half of the hurtful remarks you did say. Like, I was never the motherly type, or you were neglected! Mia you was with me every second god sent. You were never alone. You may not have had constant friends, but you had some, every stop we came to you made a friend."

"Yes Jennifer, but I had no one close to me. You were around, but you were always busy and most of the time you didn't even talk to me. Everything that went wrong for you was my fault, even if I wasn't in the room. I didn't have a childhood Jennifer, I had a job at the age of six, doing your hair and make up, because you claimed you couldn't do it yourself. I used to have to put on a deep voice on the phones if I needed to talk to you, if I was ill or something because half the people you worked with didn't even know you had a kid, so they wouldn't let me talk to you."

Jennifer looked stunned, she'd never seen me like this before, I was always so quiet and never complained. "Well thanks to you, instead of just telling me, you've told the whole bloody world, and now, I'm down as a really bad mother. If this affects the theater reviews, I could get fired!"

"Oh, I'm sorry, I forgot all about that, yes of course your job, the most important thing in the world, then it's Jim, then it's me, or is it Marie first then me, you know, I'm finding it hard to keep track. I'm sorry if what has been said hurt you, but to tell you the truth, even though I only said half of what has actually been written, it's all true, all of it. That writer really hit the nail on the head and I hope to god she gets a raise."

I will never forget the look on her face. The tears welling up in her eyes, her bottom lip quivering. The lines on her face really showed up, for the first time in her life, she looked old, like I had sucked the youth out of her. Her face goes so blotchy, when she cries, that she rarely lets herself do it. It also shows a 'weakness in character', or so she says.

"Well, I sure hope you have somewhere to stay over Christmas, because you won't be staying with me. Here." She thrust a poorly wrapped present into my hand and stomped away.

I hadn't noticed, but it had started to snow again. I looked up at the sky and blinked as a snowflake drifted into my eye. I wasn't going to cry. That women had made me cry too many times already in my life, it was over now. I was never going to cry for her again.

Chapter fourteen

Thursday afternoon and the best way to pass the time until my meeting with Doctor Grey, was writing in my journal. I could hear the girls outside, but my window was facing away from them, so I couldn't see what they were doing. I was scribbling away, when something hit the glass. Intrigued, I slipped my journal underneath my pillow and stepped up to look out. Julie had a handful of pebbles and she threw another one. One of the nurses tapped her on the hand and said something, waving her finger in the air/ I assume she was telling her off. Julie started motioning to me, to open my window.
I twisted the handle and lent out.
   "Yes?"
   "Come down here. It's a lovely day!" Julie called up.
   "No, I'm quite happy up here thank you."
Kate walked up and stood next to Julie, they were both wearing Mulan dresses and looked very pretty.
   "Come on, come down... now don't make us come up there." They both called up in unison.

"All right." I said, with a smile "I'm on my way."

They gave each other a high five and ran round the corner, out of sight. I put the new flip flops on, that Doctor Grey had bought me, the last time we went to London. I straightened my skirt out and made sure my hair was looking presentable, just in case Doctor Grey was around. I was finding myself looking for him, every time I left my room. Every time the double doors opened, at the end of the hall my heart would flutter, in the hopes that it would be him. He'd taken his annual leave this last week and I had missed him terribly. I had received a post card from him, of a little wooden house surrounded by the country side, all it said was *I promise to take you here one day. Miss you.* He hadn't signed it, but I knew it was from him. I ran my finger down the picture of the house. He promised, I thought and as yet, he's never broken a promise.

I shut the door hard behind me and looked for Chloe. We were getting on a lot better now, but I was still weary of her.

I smiled at the nurse, sitting at her station and she gave me a little wave. "Ooh, you going outside?" She asked.

"Yes, the girls want me to go out."

"I'll come with you, it's such a lovely day, and I desperately need a break." she smiled.

I love sunny days, it puts everyone it such a good mood, I thought. The nurse went ahead of me and left me to struggle with the big heavy doors.

The garden was very hushed. All I could hear were the birds chirping up in the trees. I stopped and took in a deep breath.

I followed the way the nurse went and walked round the building.

"Surprise!!!!"

My heart felt like it nearly jumped out of my mouth. The whole of my ward was in the garden. The girls, the Doctors and nurses. Balloons were hanging from the trees and there was a big banner suspended between two lamp post's reading HAPPY BIRTHDAY. I looked around at all the excited faces. So that's what they'd been doing all morning. I had actually forgotten it was my birthday, no one had said anything.

"Happy Birthday Hilary!" Every one called and Chloe walked up with a birthday cake.

"Blow them out and make a wish." She said, with excitement in her eyes.

I took in a deep breath and blew out the three candles. The cake was covered in pink icing and had '*Happy Birthday Hilary!*' Written in blue letters. "I didn't think you knew when my birthday was. Wow, thank you all so much." I felt a lump rise in my throat and tears form behind my eyes. "Thank you, thank you." I kept saying. I couldn't believe how loved I felt. A feeling I hadn't experienced in a long time, and have never experienced with so many people.

"How old are you today then Hilary?" asked Cook

"Twenty! The big two zero!"

"Finally got there then." Called out one of the girls.

"Present!" Kate shouted. Everyone agreed and was all looking very excited.

I stood, anxiously waiting. The girls parted and I saw, like an angel descending from the heavens, Doctor Grey slowly walking towards me. My chest and throat tightened with excitement, at the sight of him and an incredible feeling of relief swept over me.

"You're back." I whispered, as he pulled me into his embrace and gave me a little kiss on my lips.

"Wooooo." Chorused the girls. "Open the present!"

I hadn't even noticed the present he was holding. He handed it to me and like a child, I ripped off the wrapping paper. My eyes widened and the girls fell silent.

It was a proper Journal. The cover was made from some sort of light metal and it was full of paper to write on.

"You can add pages to it." I looked up and Chloe came forward again. "I chose it, I thought you could put the pages in you've already written and then carry on writing in there."

"Thank you." I whispered trying not to cry.

"It's engraved." Julie pipped up.

I opened the front cover and engraved on the metal plate, was written. *'For all your secrets, love from all your friends'*. A single tear, escaped my eye and I quickly wiped it away.

"Come on, lets eat." Cook called. The girls all spread out and a big table was revealed, piled high with party food. They all tucked in to the feast. I had butterflies in my tummy and couldn't face eating anything yet.

I turned back to Doctor Grey, he stood tall and strong. The country air had done him good, he looked tanned and well rested.

"You look beautiful." I whispered.

"So do you, birthday girl, you get my post card?"

"I knew that was from you."

He put his arm round me and led me to the table of food.

Moira walked over to me, after I'd finished talking to nurse Sarah. "I made this for you." And she handed me a home made card. It was pink with a white birthday cake on the front. I opened it and read the tiny writing inside. *'Happy Birthday Hilary. You are very lucky. Love from Moira and Fredrick'*.

"I'm lucky because I have such lovely friends." I smiled at her.

She looked at me sadly, "It was my birthday yesterday, but no one wished me happy birthday."

"Oh my goodness, I'm..." But before I could finish, I heard someone call my name. I turned my head to see who had spoken but, everyone was busy talking, no one was looking up at me.

"Kate told me how nice you were to her and that you helped her with something and I was just wondering, if I could talk to you."

I smiled at her and stroked her arm. "Of course, you..."

Someone calling my name, distracted me again. I looked around all the faces near to me, but still no one looked up. I turned back, to talk to Moira, but she had gone.

Every now and then, I kept seeing a face, that I knew from

somewhere. One minute she was there, the next she was gone, then I would see her again, but not long enough to focus on her face properly. She was strangely familiar, but I couldn't see her long enough to work out who she was, or where I'd seen her before. There was something about her though that made me uneasy, she seemed to move in a way that was almost ghostlike.

"Is there a new girl here?" I asked Doctor Grey, after the party had quietened down.

"No, why?"

"I keep seeing this face, I recognise her, but I don't know where from. I can't quite put my finger on it."

Doctor Grey looked round to where I was looking, then shrugged. "I don't know, sorry."

He was then called away, by one of the other Doctors and I was left alone. I felt someone looking at me and I turned my head to see where the gaze was coming from. I looked back at the last place I'd seen the lady and there she was again. This time she waved at me and beckoned me over. I put my plate down on the bench, where I was sitting and walked curiously towards her. Fear and excitement come over me at the same time. I had not had a visitor, since I'd been here. Maybe, it was a relative of mine, coming to wish me happy birthday. Oh if only.

As I approached her, I was aware that her feet were not quite touching the ground. She was solid, but she didn't seem quite there, she was flickering like a flame on a candle and coming in and out of focus like a poorly tuned television. I finally saw her face. I looked at her in amazement, it was me. The hair on my neck prickled up on its end and a shiver was sent down my spine. I looked down at my arms, they were covered in Goosebumps.

What was a beautiful warm day, suddenly turned bitterly cold. There was a strong wind blowing my hair, yet the leaves on the trees did not move. I looked around and the ground was covered in white snow. I curled my toes up to try and keep them warm. Then suddenly I was no longer at the hospital, but in the centre of London surrounded by fast cars and fast people, hurrying along to get out of the cold. I looked to my right and saw Hyde Park, then I looked to my left and I saw a tall building. I tried to digest what I was seeing. When I was last here with Doctor Grey, there was a school there. Had we gone back in time?

I strained my eyes, to see the people standing around outside the building. The women, certainly were not dressed for this weather. But then nor was I. I looked harder, as I recognised one of the women from the dream, I had had a while back. Doctor Grey described the place as a Brothel. Looking at them now, I think he was right. The women were being taken away by men and a couple of them walked into a B + B that was situated on the corner.

The lady flickered again and caught my eye.

"Who are you?" I asked her softly, studying her face.

"No. You know who I am." She paused. "But I don't think you quite know who you are."

I felt puzzled.

"I have something I need to tell you." Her voice was soft and dreamy, listening to her made me suddenly feel very sleepy. My eyes felt heavy and it was all I could do to stay standing up as my legs started collapsing beneath me.

"Please tell me." I said drearily.

"You need to give Doctor Grey your journal and he must read it. He already knows how to help you, he just doesn't know he knows. Help him by giving him your journal."

"But it's private!" I tried to protest, but I felt too weak.

"He wants to help you, it's the only way you and he can be together, please do it for all of us."

"All of us?" Then appearing beside her, was the younger version of me, still covered in blood from the waist down. The sight was chilling.

"Ok." I said feeling out of breath and rather confused. I could hear Doctor Grey calling me. I tried to answer, but no words come out. I then felt myself falling, but had no power to stop.

"You've got to understand, your past, before you can start your future."

"Got ya!" Doctor Grey said, grabbing my under arms and lowering me slowly to the ground. "What on earth were you doing?"
I quickly came to and looked around, I was back at the hospital. I felt fine, like nothing had happened at all.

"God you're freezing!" He said rubbing my arms up and down fast to try and warm them up..

"I'm ok, where did she go?" I asked quickly.

"Who Hilary?"

"That lady, I was talking to and the girl."

"I saw no lady or girl. Are you ok? You look really white."
I stood up and brushed myself off. "Yes I feel fine."

"Well, what happened?"
I explained to him what had happened and what was said. "She said to let you read my Journal and she said it would help you to help me."
He looked at me startled.

"She said that you know how to help me, but you don't know you know and that my journal will help give you answers."

"And how do you feel about giving me your journal?"

"Strangely ok, I didn't think I would be, but yeah, I'll go and get it."

"Oh." He said surprised, "Ok."
I walked past him and ran to the front door. I felt different, empowered. Something had changed within me.

"Hey, you're not going in are you? We're about to play some games."
I turned around and saw Julie looking at me hopefully.

"No, I'm just going in to get something, then I'll be straight back out, I promise."

"Ok." She said and spun around as Kate tickled her ribs, Julie screamed and chased her round the corner of the Hospital.

Chapter fifteen

It was the in middle of the afternoon and I was sat in the kitchen in my pajamas, shivering. I didn't think to go and get a jumper to put on. The snow had fallen again, and it was just as deep as before. Yesterday the city was full of people, panic buying, trying to get everything done before Christmas. I still had not got anyone any presents. The present Jennifer had given me, was still unopened, under the Fir tree, James had chopped down a few nights ago.

I ran my fingers over the scratches in the old wooden table. My head was swirling with thoughts of Jennifer and Simply Fashion magazine. I was still kicking myself for being so stupid. You would think, after all my years of dealing with people like that, through Jennifer, I would have learnt something by now. Many people have stopped me in the streets and congratulated me on such a good article, and pitying me on what a hard life I must have had. I've had radio interviewers call in asking me to go on their show. I did not ask for all that and I certainly didn't want it. Jennifer never exploited me once, apart from when I was being born, but I don't think I really minded back then. But I was still angry at the fact she got so angry. Most of what was written was true, even though I didn't say it. Why couldn't she except that she is not perfect? That she was a rubbish mother. I suppose it's hard to say you have failed, especially if you are Jennifer Preston. It had been three days since the incident with Jennifer and I was still feeling troubled.

James walked in through the front door.

"Hey, my last patient has the Flu so won't be doing him today. You still not dressed!" He said accusingly as he walked into the kitchen.

I shrugged and took another sip of coffee that Lillian had kindly, with out being asked, placed in front of me. She said she was going out and to tell James something, but I was too lost in my thoughts, that I had forgotten what that was.

"Where's Lillian?"

I shrugged in response again and took another sip, slurping loudly.

"What have you done today?"

I shook my head and shrugged my shoulders again.

"Hey!" James shouted, slamming his fist down on the table, making me jump. "Snap out of it ok! This is not your fault, nor is it Jennifer's. Now come on, it's not fair. I haven't done anything wrong either and you're treating me like *shit*!" He placed his hands firmly on his hips and waited for a response.

I didn't even look up, I didn't really want to look at him.

He huffed and put his slippers on, they were still under the table where he'd left them earlier that morning. James liked to know where they were when he got home from work, so Lillian never put them away.

"Just stop it Mia, ok? Sought yourself out!" He stormed out of the kitchen and miss judging the step, going up into the hallway, he stumbled a few steps forward and landed in a heap on the floor.

I stared in astonishment, for a moment then ran over to him to see if he was injured. "You ok?"

His body was shaking. He lifted himself up, turned and looked at me. He was laughing.

I tried to fight back the giggles, but I couldn't, I burst out laughing too.

"You looked so funny!" I laughed, now hysterically. "You looked like some dramatic scene from an amateur movie!"

He laughed harder and pulled me to the floor unexpectedly. I grabbed hold of the coat stand in surprise and brought the whole thing down with me. We lay on the floor tangled up in coats. If only there was someone else there, who could have seen us. James had my pink scarf draped over his forehead and I was entwined in Penny's lead.

We laughed even more, at the sight of each other and of how clumsy we were. I hadn't laughed in days, so was making the most of it.

We slowly calmed down, breathing deeply to try and regain control of ourselves. He turned his head and looked at me. He moved a strand of my hair that had fallen over my eyes. "You're so beautiful when you laugh. You light up the whole room."

I calmed and looked at him and he leaned forward and kissed me.

I hadn't realised, but I had been so engrossed in feeling angry and guilty, that I hadn't paid him any attention for days. I lifted my hand up and pulled his face in closer.

We made love right there on the hall floor, surrounded by coats.

* * *

"Where did Lillian say she was going?" Asked James after we had sorted the coats and ourselves out.

"I honestly can't remember."

James rolled his eyes up to the ceiling. "What good are you if you can't pass on a single message." He said good-naturedly.

I smiled and poked my tongue out at him.

"You still feeling down?"

I nodded slowly and looked dreamily out of the window.

"I have an idea." He burst out. "But you must promise me, that it will cheer you up. I've had it planned for a few days and I think now is the time."

I looked over at him questioningly. "I can't promise that. It might be a really crap idea."

James looked playfully offended. "I know this will cheer you up. Now I've wanted one for quite some time and thought that maybe we could have one together."

I froze and looked up at him. "I'm *not* having a baby!"

"No, no, no, no, no!" He repeated.

"God you sound like Jim Trott!" I exclaimed, laughing.

"No thank you, no babies just yet. Come on, get dressed and get your coat on. Let's go and change our lives *forever.*" He widened his eyes and tried to make himself sound scary.

I jumped down off the kitchen stool and headed for the bedroom.

Lillian and I had managed to get some more of my things. Marie let us in, but we had to be gone by the time Jennifer got back. Her orders, supposedly.

I slipped on my new jeans, James had bought for me, a few days ago from Selfridges, and my warmest jumper. There was a bitter wind that had picked up again and if you weren't wearing enough layers, it would rip right through you.

We tripped through Hyde Park to the shops. I was intrigued. I couldn't possibly think of what we could be getting, that according to James, was to die for.

He stopped. "Any ideas yet?"

I shook my head.

"You've got to promise me, you will be happier ok?" I slowly nodded my head, feeling uncertain.

"Good, from this moment on, I want my old Mia back."

He tilted his head down and kissed me softly on the lips. "Hey, what are you doing?" I said as he blindfolded me.

"Let me be your eyes." He slowly guided me back the way we had just come.

"Where are you taking me?"

"Shush, wait and see."

He turned me gently and I heard a door open and a bell ring. There were mysterious sounds all around me, cheeps and squeaks.

"All righ', Doctor Young?" Came a mans gruff voice. "You come for the."

James quickly hushed him quickly, before he gave the game away. "Is everything ready?"

"Yes Sir, this must be the young lady then."

I felt someone take my hand and shake it. I gave a small smile.

"Through here then miss."

James led me forward a few paces. "Happy Christmas." He said and took off my blindfold.

I blinked to adjust my eyes to the light.

The plump little man opened a metal gate in front of me. He motioned for me to step inside.

There in the corner of the room, shivering, was a very small Dalmatian puppy. My heart skipped a beat.

"'E's a li'le shy."

I looked over at James and he grinned at me. I crouched down and beckoned the Dalmatian over. He looked up at me and with his head down and tail between his legs, he cautiously walked towards me. He sniffed my outstretched hand for a while, then eventually rubbed his warm head against me and started wagging his tail. His fur was as soft as silk. He looked up at me with his beautiful brown eyes. He had four little black spots on his back and a little pink nose. Instantly I had fallen in love with him.

"'E'll ge' more spots as 'E gets olda'."

I nodded at the man with his jolly red face. He reminded me of Father Christmas. "I love him! Does he have a name?" I asked, as the puppy started getting excited and licked my hands and coat. He placed his front two paws on my thighs and looked up at me wagging his tail so vigorously that he lost his balance. I just caught him before he hit the floor and I laughed out loud. The little Dalmatian wagged his tail, even more, as if he were happy that he had made me laugh.

"Nope," Replied James with a giggle and crouched down to stroke him. "You can name him."

"Really?" I looked in to the dogs deep brown eyes and over his soft fur. A name, suitable enough for such a little thing. I thought about all the famous dogs names, from television and dog shows, but nothing fitting.

"Polo." I finally said and he wagged his tail.

"Ooh 'E likes tha'."

I picked him up under his front legs. "You coming home with us?"

He yapped in response and licked my nose.   "You sure Penny will be ok with him?"

"She will just have to get used to him, won't she. She'll be fine." James talked to the man, about what to feed him and what injections he'd had, whilst I chose Polo a new collar and lead.

"Thank you so much, I never expected this."

James put his arm around me and gave me a squeeze.

The man opened the door and the cold winter came rushing into the shop. Polo sniffed the snow and backed off back into the pet shop.

"We'll probably have to carry him." Said James.

I bent down and picked him up. He was shaking from the cold.

"Hold on a minute." James went back into the shop.

Wrapping my arms around his little quivering body, I held Polo closer to keep him and myself warm.

James came back out holding a little brown bag.

"What's in there?" I asked.

"Watch."

I watched him put a little blue and Grey woolen coat over Polo and rub him to warm him up.

"Oh how sweet." I said giving James a kiss. Then I gave Polo one. "My two best boys." I said and rubbed my head into Polo's.

We walked home as quickly as we could. There was a cruel wind and it bit at our nose and ears. The snow was getting deeper and our feet sank into the soft snow with every step we took, which made the journey home, a lot harder.

I'd never had a pet before. It would have been unfair, because of all our moving about. But what was extra special was, that Polo was James' and mine.

Polo buried his head into my coat and his hot breath kept me warm.

Chapter Sixteen

The past problems, with Chloe and I, had completely vanished. We were becoming really good friends now. She had a wicked sense of humor and could make me laugh, just by laughing herself. She still spoke her mind, but it wasn't so aggressive with what she had to say and the girls took less offense. She confided in me, about all her suicide attempts and what her life was like before she had come to the hospital. She told me how she had been in the ward below us, where the clinically depressed and really mentally unstable patients go. She had to prove to her doctor that she was no longer depressed or suicidal and that she could control her anger, so she could come up stairs to this ward.

"What's so good about this ward?" I asked.

"This ward is your ticket out of here. If you're up here, you're on your way home."

"But what about Kate and Julie and Moira?"

"They'll get homes to go to. They're no threat to themselves, or anyone else, so they are on their way home. That's why you're up here now, you're no longer a threat to yourself."

"No longer?"

"No, you were, but now you are so much better. It took a while, but you got there."

I thought a lot about what Chloe had said, so one day whilst we were in my bedroom, enjoying the chocolates her cousin had brought her, I decided, now was the time to ask her what she had meant.

"A few days ago, you said about me being a danger to myself. What did you mean by that?"

Chloe stopped chewing and looked at me perplexed.

"Oh nothing." She said shaking her head and braking off another piece. "Want some more?"

"No thank you. It did mean something, something that you're not allowed to say, maybe. Please tell me."

Chloe swallowed hard.

"Now, you know how much I like a good scandal. But this, this is really nothing to do with me. You need to talk to Doctor Grey about this."

I looked at her, I could see by the expression on her face, she was not going to tell me.

"Tell you what though, I think you should make your journal into a book. It's really interesting."

I smiled coyly.

"If you don't mind me asking. Did you really do all that stuff and go to all those places?" She sounded doubtful. "And your mother!"

The question made me feel very anxious. I didn't really like talking about her. "Well yes." I replied cautiously. I flicked a few crumbs of chocolate off my bed and looked out of the window.

"What's wrong, have I said something I shouldn't?"

"No you haven't, don't worry." I took another piece of chocolate.

"So after that incident with your mum, is that when they put you in here?"

I remembered that day of the fire so well. The memory still sent chills down my spin. "Yes it was."

"What happened with that man you were seeing, where did he go?"

"I don't know. I have no memory past that day. They say I had a nervous brake down. I don't even remember coming here."

"That's sad. I'm sorry."

"Don't be."

She tilted her head and smiled, then poked her tongue out at me. I tried not to giggle but couldn't help it.

"I'm glad you're in here. I'm feeling a lot better because of you, thank you."

I smiled. "You have no idea how much you're helping me, too."

She grinned back and laughed at the funny face she was pulling. It was hard to believe that this girl, could ever want to commit suicide. She was so full of life.

* * *

My tummy was rumbling. Dinner had been called half an hour ago, but at the time I was not hungry.

The day was cold, nothing like my birthday when the sun was blazing, with a little light breeze to help keep you cool. Today it was gray, with threatening black clouds. The air outside was very thick and close. It seemed hard to take in a good full breath.

I put on my old thick woolly jumper. The heating wasn't on during the day in the summer so the corridors were cold. For the first time in weeks, I was wearing jeans and my trainers.

I stepped out of my room and locked the door behind me. The place was quiet, all the girls and staff must have been in the dinner hall. I shoved my hands in my sleeve and started up the corridor but something caught my attention. I looked down the corridor towards the offices at the end and standing at the front desk was Doctor Grey talking to a woman. Curiosity got the better of me. I walked slowly towards the double doors at the end and hid myself next to the wall. I tilted my head around so I could see what was happening.

The women was pretty, she had short black hair that was styled in a chopping sought of fashion. She was a lot taller than me and just a little smaller that Doctor Grey. She was slender and had an air of confidence in the way she held herself.

Doctor Grey brought out a file that he had tucked under his arm and opened it. The women looked over and put her hand to her mouth. Her eyes filled with tears and she nodded her head in response to what ever Doctor Grey had said. He placed his hand gently on her arm and she moved in to him and buried her head in his shoulder.

A twinge of jealousy took hold of me.

The woman then moved her head in my direction and I quickly hid. I took in a deep breath of shock, the look in her eyes, that sad hurt look reminded me of someone. God I wish I could remember who.

I suddenly felt sad for her. Why did she look in so much pain? Yet she had a far off look of relief in her eyes.

I moved my head back round and Doctor Grey looked right at me. The woman saw me as well and took a few steps towards me but Doctor Grey stopped her. I waved, slightly embarrassed and lent back against the wall. "Busted!" I thought.

A few moments later the door opened and Doctor Grey walked in. He swiveled around and gave me a cheeky grin.

"Eavesdropping?"

"No, I couldn't hear you." I said, sounding a little too disappointed. "Who was she?"

He smiled at me with an accomplished look on his face.

"Her name is Rene Marks and she has just discovered that a member of her family, who she has been looking for for years, is in this hospital."

"Oh?"

"She thought she'd never see them again."

"Wow. I recognize her from somewhere."

"Do you? Well, when she saw you then, she said she'd like to meet you."

"Really? Wow, I've never had a visitor. Why does she want to meet me?"

"Because you may know who she's been looking for and she wants to talk to you about them."

I didn't feel I needed to question that, I was just glad that I was going to have my first visitor.

He put his arms around me and pulled me in close to him. "When can I see you again? It seems like it's been forever."

"Well how about now?"

He smiled and quickly led me into his office. He shut the door behind me and pressed me up against it.

"God, I missed you!" He said between kisses.

It felt so good being with him again.

"When can we make love?" He asked softly.

The words tightened my chest and gave me butterflies in my stomach. But I knew we couldn't yet. Not until I was out of the hospital.

"Soon." I whispered. "When I'm out of here."

"Really, well that's not going to be too long now. I've finished your journal and I'm doing some research on names and places that you've written down, it's looking hopeful."

"Oh wow! Well it's nice that you've read my deepest darkest thoughts and you still want to make love to me."

"Oh yeah!" He kissed me again passionately and I could feel every ounce of him enjoying me.

"I love you." He said softly.

I stopped kissing him and bent my head back away from him.

"Pardon?"

"I said, I love you."

"Wow!" I kissed him hard and he stumbled backwards onto his desk.

"Ok, we can't kiss like that, if we're not going to go all the way..."

I smiled at him. "Ok." I pulled his tie down to bring him closer to me and whispered "I love you too and I promise as soon as I'm out of here..." I stopped and bit my lower lip and walked towards the door.

"You're so naughty." He said frustrated.

I turned back and winked at him, as I closed the door behind me.

* * *

"Where have you been?" Chloe demanded as I entered the dinning hall. Her face was white and her eyes wide.

"Why, did you miss me?"

"Have you seen Doctor Grey?" A nurse interrupted.

"I think he's in his office, why?"

Without answering she quickly left the room.

I looked around at all the girls. They were all ashen faced and red eyed. "What?" I asked quietly then I looked over at our usual table. Moira's seat was empty. "Where's Moira?" I asked. I looked at Julie, who was sat with a look of despair in her eyes. She was looking far away, beyond the walls of the hospital, somewhere where no one could reach her.

I looked around. No one answered, but a few of the girls looked out across the hall and into Moira's' room.

I walked out of the room and into her bedroom.

"No, don't!" Forewarned Chloe. But she didn't try to stop me.

I curiously pushed the door open slowly and gasped in horror at the sight that was before me. Hanging from a beam with a yellow scarf digging in around her neck was Moirés little body. She was only a few inches off the ground. If she was a little bit taller, she would have touched the floor. The chair lay on its side. Her head was limp and had fallen to one side and her brown hair was tied up in a ponytail. Her Face was tear stained. She was dressed in her pink rabbit pajamas and one of her slippers had fallen off her foot and she had gripped in her hand the poor Fredrick.

I clapped my hands to my mouth and let out a faint whimper. I lent back against the opened door, my legs went from beneath me and I slipped down.

The world started spinning. I could feel my heart pounding in my chest, I felt nauseous and my whole body shook.

Doctor Grey came running in and stopped suddenly at the sight of her. He stood motionless for a few moments. He then turned around and saw me huddled on the floor. I looked up at is waxen face.

"Get her out of here." He commanded one of the nurses and Sarah helped me to my feet.

"Come on Hun' lets get you something to eat."

"Why did she, why would she do that?"

Without answering Sarah took me into the dinner hall with the other girls and sat me down on one of the chairs. My body was shaking from shock. Julie and Kate ran over to me and knelt down beside me burying their heads in my lap.

"Why is she still hanging there?" I asked softly between sobs.

"They can't take her down till they've examined everything. Checked that it was suicide and all that."

I looked up at Chloe. "Oh she wanted me to help her." I sobbed, remembering our short conversation we had had on my birthday. "She asked me on my birthday to help her with something but I got distracted. Oh god I should have listened. I should have taken care of her." I cried, grief taking over my whole being.

Chloe put her arms around my neck and rocking me slowly, we all wept.

Chapter seventeen

I closed my eyes and slowly sank my whole body into the warm water. I heard it rise up over my ears and I felt my hair drift around me. I couldn't hear a sound apart from my own heart beating in my ears. I blew out as much air as I could and my body sank to the bottom of the bath. I lay there still for a while, not thinking, not moving. Until I felt like, if I did not come up for air now, I would never need to again. I lifted my head up out of the water and took in an almighty breath. Polo was there to greet me. He licked the water of my face then got distract by Penny, who was sitting in the doorway. I laid against the towel, that was hanging over the bath to support my back and watched Polo and Penny play, considering the whole cat and dog rivalry theory they got on significantly well. Polo had only been with us two days but he had already settled in. I reached for the soap and washed my face. I thought about James. Being my new boyfriend he was in my thoughts a lot. I thought about his brylcreem hair without a strand out of place, the way he dresses so nicely, even when he was in casuals he still looked nice. That's the thing about having a lot of money, you can afford to look nice, even when you don't have to. Every time we go out he always wears his suit. He only ever wears jeans or sweats when we're at home. Lillian calls him old fashioned, but I think he's charming.

I lifted my leg up out of the water, to check if I needed to shave. I had waxed a week ago and luckily, it still hadn't grown back.

I thought for a moment about James' parents. They died so suddenly and unexpected. I never even knew my father. According to Jennifer he died before I was born. He left her with a load of money and that helped her towards stardom. I had asked her once, if she was sure that that money wasn't meant for me. She said no and that he died before either of them knew she was pregnant. I'd like to believe that, but from past experiences with Jennifer I wasn't to sure. Then without warning I got an over whelming sense of missing her. Thinking about how James is never going to see his mother again, because of one of life's cruelties. Yet I won't, because we're both so stubborn. I should call her I thought, but like most of my thoughts they slowly disappear until they are forgotten.

"I'm home!" James called up the stairs.

"I'm in the bath, care to join me?"

"Hell yeah!"

I heard James feet pound up the stairs and across the landing. "What have we got today then? Lavender, or..." He reached out for the half full bubble bath bottle on the side of the bath. "White Peony. Interesting."

He quickly undressed and carefully got into the bath. "Goodness, why do you have the bath so hot, you ever want children?"

I smirked at him and flicked him with water.

"You know what today is?"

"No, what's today?"

He leaned in closer, as if it were a secret. "It's our one month anniversary."

"Wow, really?"

"Yep, we met in the coffee shop this day one month ago and to celebrate I have taken the liberty to make dinner reservations for... guess."

I thought for a moment. "I have no idea." I shook my head.

"The Ritz!"

I nearly slipped under the water in my excitement. "Really!?"

He nodded proudly.

"Jennifer always talks about her time spent at the Ritz Hotel, but I've never been. Are we going to stay the night too?"

"Do you want to stay the night?"

"Oh yes please!"

"Then stay the night, we shall."

I quickly washed the rest of my body and jumped out of the bath, so James had more space to wash his hair.

"But, I have nothing to wear." I said in dismay.

"Oh I'm sure you'll find something."

Yeah right, I thought, I've never owned anything worth wearing to a place like The Ritz Hotel. I dried myself and dropped my towel untidily on the bed. I walked across the room to the wardrobe, James had made room for some of my dresses, but they were all summery dresses, made out of cheesecloth material and had big flower patterns. I may look nice, but not' Ritzy' nice. Then something stuck out at me. I saw a white tag with Miss Galliano printed on the label. My heart skipped little beats of excitement. I tenderly pulled out the hanger and with it came a long silk black dress. It had a tie up back like one of Jennifer's night gowns and a small flower made out of the dress material on the left shoulder then had silk ribbon running down to the hem. I put the dress up to myself and looked in the mirror. It finished way above my knee. A garment Jennifer would never approve of, if she saw it. I then saw something I didn't see before in the corner of the room, by the wardrobe was a black box that had the name, Faith, printed on the top and sides. I tenderly laid the dress down on the bed, walked over and opened the box. Inside was a pair of black strapped shoes with a four-inch heel and a dainty curved toe. I thought I would die of excitement. I put the dress and shoes on slowly, to savor every moment. James walked into the room, just as I was tying up the back of the dress.

"Need help?"

"No." I replied. "Have been doing things like this all my life." I twirled round, so James could see all of me.

"You look beautiful." He said softly.

"Thank you so much, it's perfect."

He walked over and kissed me softly. He ran his hands down my back and lifted up my dress.

"You're not wearing underwear!" He exclaimed as he caressed my buttocks with his fingers.

"No, I haven't put any on yet."

"Don't." He whispered and kissed me.

*   *   *

The Restaurant was beautiful. A kind looking waiter showed us to our table. We were sat in the corner, where it was private and we could talk.

"How did we manage to get such a good table?" I asked looking around the room.

"You have to book well in advance."

I looked at him curiously. "How did you mange that? We've only been together a month."

"I booked it that day we met at the Coffee shop. I made a promise to myself that one way or another, this time next month, you will be sitting here next to me."

"That's very confident of you James. What would you have done, if it didn't work and I had wanted nothing to do with you."

"But you did want something to do with me, didn't you!" He smiled triumphantly. "Well if you hadn't come, I probably would have brought Lillian."

I giggled. "She's like your surrogate mum, isn't she."

"Well yes. She used to live in the part of the house, that is now cut off, my dad hired her to help my mum, after I was born and after my parents died, her and her husband looked after me, till I was old enough to look after myself." James paused. "Did I tell you about my parents?"

I panicked, I didn't want to get Lillian into any trouble for telling me. But then I could never imagine James ever getting that angry. "I accidentally came upon your parents study and Lillian explained what had happened."

He nodded his head in response and his eyes scanned his menu. I felt he was trying to distract himself from our conversation. I felt a tension start to rise, like a big cloud had formed over our table.

"So Lillian is married?" I asked, out of curiosity, but also to take the subject off death.

"No." James sadly shook his head. "He died of cancer last year."

"Oh my god, I'm sorry. That's awful." Well so much for taking the conversation away from death.

"That's ok. So what are you going to have?"

I looked down at my menu. I nearly fainted at the sight of the prices. "It's so expensive."

"Don't worry, I'll just re-mortgage the house." He laughed at his little joke. "Have anything you want."

At that moment our waiter came to the table.

"What will it be tonight Sir?" He asked, looking at James.

"Um, my usual please Martin."

"The Sirloin, excellent choice Sir, and you miss?"

The waiter looked over at me, patiently. I tried not to laugh. I'd never heard a waiter sound so polite, or as well spoken as he was. My eyes wondered down each meal. Each dish sounding tastier then the one before it. "I'll have the Roast Duck please."

140

"Excellent choice miss and to drink?"

"Your best wine please Martin."

"Of course Sir."

I looked at James impressed. "My usual, please Martin." I imitated him. "How often do you come here?"

"Not very, but I always make sure, Martin is my waiter, he is the best. The first time I came in here, was after my split with Claire, he served me. The next time, was three months later and he served me again. He remembered my name and what I ordered before, everything."

"Wow, impressive."

"He likes me, because I give him such a good tip."

Our food arrived half an hour later. Unlike other restaurants, I had been to in the past, the food filled up the whole plate, instead of a little pile in the middle. It really was a feast.

Martin placed the ice bucket down and showed us the wine, like they do in the movies.

He poured us a glass each, bowed and left us to our meal.

I looked up the wine in the menu. "Penfolds Grange Hermitage South Australia 1960 £500. Are ya kidding me!"

James had already tucked into his meal. "What? It's nice wine!"

"It better be."

"You ever had good expensive wine before?"

I remembered the first time and the last time, I ever drank, was on my eighteenth birthday. I got absolutely plastered off Appletinis. A performance, I never wish to give again. Jennifer still hasn't let me live it down. All I can remember is a clown a broom and the beach. I was told I was still a virgin, when I woke up but it still has a question mark over it. "No, never had wine before."

"Well you're going to love this. Lets make a toast."

We raised our glasses together. "To us." James said.

"To us." I repeated and we clinked glasses.

I took a sip. It was a full bodied wine, sweet and bitter. I could taste a hint of mint, caramel and sweet cherry, all present at the same time. I'm no wine taster, but it was absolutely beautiful.

We must have sat there talking, eating and drinking for at least three hours. The effects of the wine did not really hit me, until I stood up to go to the bathroom. I excused myself and tried desperately to walk in a straight line, to the end of the restaurant. I tried to walk sexy, swing my hips, just in case James was watching but instead, I ended up careering into Martin, who took me by the arm and escorted me out.

"Off to the bathroom miss?"

"I fink so." I slurred.

"May I be your guide miss?"

"I'd love you to Martin." I giggled. That's why I didn't drink. I was such a flirt.

"You know, yourrr very hansom for an older man."

"Thank you miss, my wife thinks so too."

I giggled even more as he practically carried me down the stairs.

"You soo nice!" I lent on what I though was a solidly, closed door but it swung open as I lent on it. I fell, stumbling into the men's room. Martin tried to catch me but, missed. My legs spread apart, as I fell and the men doing their business got a full view of, an idea James thought would be really sexy. I picked myself up off the floor, with Martins help. I looked at the astonished men, I'm sure one of them was Kevin Costner, but then I was severely drunk.

"Nice th,thing." I stammered, smiling at the stranger.

Martin quickly ushered me out.

"Same to you." The man called as the door closed. I laughed hysterically.

"Miss Preston, you need to calm down, otherwise I am going to have to ask you to leave and I don't want to do that as James is a valued costumer."

I surprisingly understood what he meant and straightened myself up. "Where are the Ladies?"

"In here miss." I stumbled in and managed to do what I needed to do.

I swung the door open and James stood in the hallway looking magnificent.

"You look like a dream."

"And you look like a drunk." He replied catching me as I fell.

"Shhhh, otherwise Martin will kick us out." I whispered.

James sat me down and handed me a glass of water.

"Sip it slowly."

We sat there for a few minutes in silence. I slowly sipped my water like he'd asked. "I'm sorry. I've ruined the evening."

"No, not at all. It was my fault, really. I shouldn't have kept pouring you glass after glass." He lent over and kissed my forehead.

The men's bathroom door swung open and out stepped the gentlemen I had complimented.

"Hey, pretty lady." He was American, so he pronounced it Preddy, and winked at me, as he walked past.

"Who was that?" James asked.

"My friend." I replied and sunk my face into his shoulder.

Chapter eighteen

I sat in front of the mirror in my bedroom. Tears were still running down my cheeks. No matter how many times I had wiped them away, they just kept on falling.

Moira's' funereal was beautiful. We had it in the hospital chapel. A few members of her extended family were there, but it was mostly the girls from the ward, that took up most of the seats. A strange man I had never seen before spoke. But he didn't really know much about Moira, I probably knew more and that was even more upsetting.

There was a little knock at the door.

"Come in." I called and wiped away another tear.

The door slowly opened and Kate stuck her little head through. "Can I come in, please?"

"Of course!" I quickly jumped up out of my seat and pulled the chair round for her to sit on.

We sat in silence for a while, until Kate said. "That could have been me up there?"

"Up where?"

"Hanging." She looked down at the picture in her hand.

"What, why?" I asked, fearful for whatever the answer may have been.

"You remember that day, when you found this and you held me whilst I cried?" She said, giving the photograph of her and her father a little wave.

I nodded.

"I was thinking of, well you know, that day."

"Why?" I tried to keep my voice calm and steady, she was being so blunt.

"No one really talks to me. Yeah Julie is fun to play with, but she doesn't listen to me. When you held me tight it made everything seem ok again. Hilary you saved my life."

Another tear rolled down my cheek, but not for Moira, for Kate. There was such pain in the world, especially in this hospital. You think people in here need Doctors and psychiatrists, but what they really need are friends.

"Thank you Kate. But, I blame myself for Moira's death. I should have done the same for her as I did for you. She needed me."

"It's not up to you to save everybody. God would never put such a big burden on such a small persons shoulders. It's all the little things you do that make a difference."

"Yes, but not for Moira."

"We all did what we could. If you were distracted maybe that was for your own good."

Wow, I thought. Such wisdom from a 'seven' year old. They didn't give her enough credit.

"Oh, and thanks to Moira, she made me realise that I've been in here long enough, there is more to life than staring out of windows. If I'm meant to see Father Christmas, he'll come to me. I've spoken to Doctor Grey and I'm leaving next month. He's found a family for me." She stood up and smiled. She bent down and kissed my cheek then without another word she left.

* * *

"Hilary?"

I turned around and Doctor Grey stood in the doorway. He was so tall that the top of his hair nearly touched the door frame. He looked as beautiful as ever.

"Your visitor's here."

All the girls in the room stopped what they were doing and looked up. I followed Doctor Grey through to his office and the girls clustered around to try and see whom my visitor was. I was just as intrigued myself.

"Hello, Hilary is it?" The Woman that I had first seen in the corridor put her hand out for me to shake.

I took it. "Wow it's a pleasure to meet you. I'm so pleased you wanted to see me. You're my first ever visitor."

The woman smiled "I'm Rene Marks."

"Yes Doctor Grey told me your name."

"Please sit down." Doctor Grey motioned to his to two, tree coloured chairs.

Rene sat down so elegantly, she had such poise.

The rooms' air felt thick, like it was full of secrets. I sat down as elegantly as I could. This woman was incredibly beautiful and I felt slightly aware that I was sitting next to her and Doctor Grey was looking at both of us. I do hope he's not comparing I thought, because I really wouldn't come out well. Though I do think Rene is a bit older than Doctor Grey. Why am I worrying about that, this women needed to talk to me. I turned to her so she knew she had my full attention.

"So tell me a bit about yourself Hilary."

I didn't really know what to tell her. I'd never been asked that question before by any one apart from Doctor Grey. She didn't want to know about my life so she can put it down in some report. She really wanted to know about me. But all of a sudden my life seemed so uninteresting.

"Um, Well, My name is Hillary Jacobs, I was born in London on June first." I stopped when I saw her face. She looked away suddenly and took in a deep breath. Did I say something wrong?

"You ok?" Doctor Grey looked at her concerned.

She bit her two lips together like I do, when I'm feeling insecure and nodded her head. She looked back at me and I saw a flash of myself looking back. I shook to get the image out of my head.

"So how long have you been at this hospital?"

"I don't know exactly." I looked at Doctor Grey for help but he didn't move. "So do I know your relative who is here? hope you don't mind, but I asked and Doctor Grey told me."

"No I don't mind. Yes you do know them, quite well."

"Well who is she?"

"Who is she?" Rene repeated. "You don't know?"

A rush of dread came over me. I felt uncomfortable. Please don't let it have been Moira. I didn't want to be in that room anymore. A sickening feeling rose up in my throat, I hadn't seen her at the funeral. "Not Moira!"

"No, no. Not Moira, Hilary, don't worry." Doctor Grey cut in.

I felt a sense of relief, but even though we were talking, I didn't feel that a lot was being said and it was making me feel frustrated.

"Well then who?"

I think Doctor Grey could sense I was getting cross. He walked around his desk and crouched down beside me. He took my hands in his and

fiddled with my fingers tenderly. "You're ok Hilary. You can leave if you want to. But if you stay you must listen with an open mind." He gave my hand a squeeze, stood back up and walked over to his side of the desk. He didn't sit down he just rested his hands on the back of his chair. I could feel he was uncomfortable which made it a lot harder for me.

"Ok, look. You said you recognize Rene, well do you?" He asked finally.

Rene looked at Doctor Grey then at me. Doctor Grey shrugged as if admitting defeat. "I want to help you Hilary, please let me."

"Do you, do you recognize this man and women?"

I took the picture Rene had fished out of her bag and examined it.

"Well that's, that's me."

"No Hilary, That's your mother. You look very much like her don't you?"

I stared hard at the picture, she looked very different to the one I had in my bedroom. Here she had very high cheek bones and her nose was slightly bigger.

"So this, this must be my father. I've never seen a picture of him before. She never talked about him."

"Who, who didn't?" Rene asked me, but looked at Doctor Grey.

"My mother."

"Why not?"

"I don't know, think it was too painful for here. Anyway why do you have a picture of them?"

"Because." Rene stopped and looked up at Doctor Grey again. I could see she was hurting.

"Do you know my parents?"

She looked at me. "Yes, because they are my parents too."

"Hu?" I felt my pulse start to race, and my palms began to sweat. There was a high pitch screaming in my ears saying *run, run away.* But I couldn't, I don't think my legs could have carried me just then.

"They are my parents too." She repeated.

"Yeah I heard you the first time, what do you mean, your parents too? I was an only child."

"No, no you weren't. I'm eight years older than you. We used to be identical when we were little. Do you remember? Mama used to dress us up in the same outfits, the only difference was, was that I was always a foot taller. Still am by the looks of it." She whispered a smile.

"Is this some sought of con? I don't remember that, because it never happened, I was an only child and you are way to old to be only eight years older than me." I handed Rene back the picture. "I don't know where you got that photograph from, but…"

"I didn't come here for you to get angry with me. Ok? I came here so you can find out the truth. I have been looking for you, ever since you ran away." She shook her head in dismay and lowered her voice to a soft whisper. "It is just a relief to know you're alive. So lets just leave it at that." She wiped away the single tear that had rolled down her cheek and a green emerald ring on her ring finger caught my eye. I quickly grabbed it, taking her by surprise.

"Hey, I know this ring, It was my mothers." I looked into her eyes, at first I felt angry, maybe she had stolen it, but then something about the way she looked back at me made me soften. "Hey…" I started to say but stopped. Her eyes were familiar, they were a deep green and they seemed to go on for forever. She had a beautifully formed mouth, a big bottom lip and a delicate M shape on the top. Just like my mothers and mine. Little snippets of her started to form in my mind. I saw her as a young girl holding her hand out for me to take, her smile made me feel safe and loved.

"…I know you!"

Chapter nineteen

I sat on the edge of the bed. My head was spinning and my ears buzzing. James had managed to sober me up a little bit last night and I did manage some chocolate for pudding. We hadn't stayed in the hotel because James thought it best we went home. He hadn't asked about the man in the bathroom again, which was a relief. I was felt ashamed. My body ached from the rampant night we had had. I put my hands either side of me and hoisted myself up, I felt something under my right hand. It was a note. *Sorry I've had to go so early, emergency at work, will be back before dinner.* It was signed with kisses.
I looked down at my naked body. I had Goosebumps all over. God it was cold. I grabbed James' dressing gown and slipped my arms through. I skipped down stairs to make myself some breakfast.
   "Hello there!"
I froze in the kitchen doorway.
   "James said I would meet ya, but I didn't think I'd meet so much of ya."

I stared at the stranger mystified, then realized what he had meant. I hadn't tied the gown up around my body and I was wearing nothing underneath.

"Oh my god!" I said covering myself up.

The stranger walked towards and reached out for my hand.

"I'm Justin, how do ya do." He was American. Very tall like James with the same dark hair. He had a smile that would make any single, available girl go weak at the knees.

I put my hand in his and he shook it. "I'm Mia."

"Hello Mia." He pronounced it Meea. "I'm sorry, but I can still see a nipple."

I quickly covered myself up. I could feel my blood rise to my face. Don't go red. Don't go red, I pleaded to myself.

"Would you like some eggs?"

"Yes please."

I perched myself on the breakfast bar stool and flicked through today's paper. *Jennifer Preston quits the theatre after breakup with daughter.* Oh no. I thought, another ploy. I read on. *After the brake up with daughter Mia Preston, also well known as 'The Bathroom Baby', Jennifer says she is going on strike and won't be back until they have sorted things out between them.*

"God, she's desperate!" I said aloud.

"Who?" Justin replied carrying my egg on toast over and placed it on the table in front of me.

"My mother." I slid the newspaper over to him so he could read it and I stood up and flicked the kettle on.

"You're The Bathroom Baby? I went to see your mother in concert when she was a singer, just before she joined the theater. She was awesome."

I smiled and shrugged my shoulders.

"So why you two not talking?"

I looked at him and realized that I didn't know who he was. He could be some stranger off the street. "I'm sorry. Who are you?"

"Justin, I did say. Didn't I?"

"Yes I know your name, but how do you know James, and what are you doing here?"

"Oh, I'm sorry, I'm James' cousin, my family moved out to America when I was five. I'm over here on business and staying with you guys for a while. That ok?"

It wasn't up to me, it was James house, but you would have thought he could have forewarned me.

I simply smiled at him and congratulated him on such a nice breakfast. I went upstairs and started to run myself a bath. I sat on the step by the side of the bath and waited for the hot water, but it didn't come. I went down the stair to check the heating, it was switched on. "Why is there no hot water?" I asked Justin.

"Oh sorry, I'd been on the plane for at least twenty one hours. So I had a nice long shower this morning. I assume James had one as well. Sorry Mia."

"That's ok, I'll just wait for it to heat back up." Justin handed me a black coffee. I thanked him and strolled up stairs to get dressed. I appreciated the coffee, should help with my hangover. I sat on the bed after I had dressed myself, not really knowing what to do, when Polo ran in with his tail wagging. He jumped on me and we rolled around on the bed for a while. He loved it when I hid my head under the blanket then jumped out and shouted Boo. He was always so surprised. "You wanna walk, do you, you want to go for a walk?" I cooed, ruffling his ears. He went crazy and ran down the stairs followed close behind by Penny. It felt very odd walking Polo *and* Penny together. I get the most strangest looks.

Justin was still in the kitchen pottering over the dishes. "Where do you keep the washing up soap?"

I pointed to the soup dispenser above the tap. He looked confused, so I walked over and pressed the button on the top and the liquid soap flopped into the washing up bowl.

"And you're from America!" I said Good-naturedly.

He smiled and poured the boiling water from the kettle into the bowl then added the cold from the tap.

Walking through the Park, I got more odd looks than usual. It was Christmas eve and people were very busy doing last minute shopping, yet they still had time to scowl and shake their heads at me as if I was a some naughty school girl who had been caught smoking behind the bike shed. The sixth time it happened I stopped the man shaking his head at me and asked, feeling cross now. "Excuse, but what is your problem with me?"

"You don't get it do you?" He said assuming I knew what he was talking about. "We love her and now look at what's happened." He gave me his newspaper, "Sought it out." He said and walked away. It was the same paper I had read at breakfast.

"It's not my fault she's being so petty!" He must have heard, I said it loud enough, but he chose to ignore me. I let Polo and penny do their business' and then stormed back home.

James was back and he apologized for Justin and said he'd forgotten all about it. I told him about the newspaper and the man in the park. "It's like I've killed her or something."

"Oh, talking about your *marm*, you received this while you were out." Justin handed an envelope to me and I handed it to James.

"You read it please. I'm too cross. You'll see it in a better light than I will at the moment."

I made myself another strong coffee and stomped into the living room to watch some daytime TV.

Our presents had already been stacked high under the Christmas tree and a twinge of excitement replaced me anger upon looking at them. I loved Christmas, but then my heart sank. I didn't want to seem nasty, but I hoped Justin had somewhere to go Christmas day. I wanted to spend it with James, Lillian had kindly gone to see her sister so we could be alone together.

"Ya don't want on old women hanging around ya, and I don't think I wanna be around you, not with all ya swooning." She had said with a smile.

James came in and I moved my legs, so he could sit down next to me. I then placed my legs on his lap.

"You better read this."

"What does it say?"

He told me how Jennifer had been to Simply Fashion and has demanded them to write an article that was factual or she would sue them if they declined.

They need you to sign it so it's legal and they can print it.

"They didn't ask me to sign the last one!" I snapped, not at him, but the situation.

"Hence the suing part."

"I'm not signing anything." I said and crossed my arms.

"Mia just read the article. You may feel differently afterwards." He lent over with the letter in his hand, I didn't move. "Mia, she's your mother. Take it."

He was right, but then he was so wise that he was always right. I took the letter from him and turned on the light above my head so I could read it clearly. It read;

When I gave birth to Mia Preston, she was 6 pounds in weight exactly. She had beautiful thick blonde hair and a gorgeous button nose. She was born on first June 1986. She pride herself on that that is the same day as Marilyn Monroe.

Mia traveled around with me everywhere. I was thinking of having her adopted at the time but couldn't face the thought of someone else looking after my beautiful little girl. So when she was at the school age I hired a private tutor for where ever we were. It was hard because she didn't have the consistency and I appreciate that now, but it was either that or boarding school and she begged me not to send her to one, so I didn't. I paid the extra expense for a tutor. Mia had a nanny until she was ten who went everywhere with us. They were good friends and I was jealous of the times Mia would be playing with her nanny whilst I had to work. In my free time we would play a lot, she found it easy making friends but until she had I would be her playmate. We would have great fun together acting out scenes from a play I was doing. We would make it very dramatic and funny and we would laugh for hours afterwards.

I didn't make Mia do my make up and hair because she was cheap, but because she was so good at it. The precision she had was incredible, she had ideas for every occasion, and for every character I played. I envied her for having such a good eye.

When she was eleven we were staying in France, we were there for a year and Mia had her first little boyfriend. He was the son of one of the other actors and would come to many rehearsals. They would play together back stage, making a total nuisance of themselves, but she was happy and I think it was with him that she shared her first kiss and now she has a lovely boyfriend who I hope will cherish her and look after her. Not that she needs much looking after, she is very head strong.

I tried my best to be a good mother. Maybe I was selfish but never neglectful. There are some mothers in the world that stay at home twenty-four seven with their children and spend less quality time with them than I did with Mia.

I am sorry if she is offended and feels unloved. Even though I never really said it, I hope she knows that I love her and always will, in life and in death, She will always be my special little girl.

I was stunned. I never knew she was so deep. Most of the things about my childhood, like the French boyfriend, I only remember now she'd said it and acting out her script together, I now remembered that too.

"Have I been unfair?" I looked at James through clouded eyes.

He sat closer and put his arm around me.

"No, you acted just like any other daughter would, and she like any other mother. She's righted the wrong and all that is needed now is an apology from both of you."

He kissed my soggy cheek and handed me a pen. "Sign it Mia."

I took the pen and signed on the designated area. I could just read my signature through my tears. James reached over my legs and handed me the cordless phone.

I dialed Jennifer's phone number. It rang for a while, then Marie picked up the other end.

"Hello, Marie. Is Jennifer there?"

"No Mia she's nota. You got a nerve ringing here." Came her nasty reply.

"Please Marie, is she there? I just want to talk to her."

There was a moment pause. I swear, I could hear Jennifer whispering in the back ground.

"No she's nota." With that Marie slammed the phone down, making me jump.

"I know she's there. I heard her, she just doesn't want to talk to me." I sobbed.

James gave me a kind smile and pulled me into him. He held me tight, whilst I sobbed. He didn't say a word, he just let me cry. Cry for the past, that I had forgotten. Cry for the mother, I may have lost, but mostly cry for myself. Crying, that maybe next time, I won't be so stupid and thoughtless. It looks like feeling sorry for myself, is the only thing I seem to be able to do.

Chapter twenty

A few days had passed since I had my visitor. After I had realized that I knew Rene from somewhere, like a cowered, I ran out of the office. I was being taken out of my comfort zone and I hated it. I was feeling so many different emotions, so many feelings that I didn't know what to do with them.

 Doctor Grey hadn't seen me since that day. I had asked the nurse why and she had said that instead of our extra meetings he was busy doing research so he can help me some more. She said the dedication he is putting into me was astounding.

I missed my journal, when I felt insecure I would read it so I could remember who I was. Also after what Chloe had said about writing it down as a book I was even more interested in my words and how I could go about it. Then thinking of Chloe made me remember something, the way she spoke that day, as if she knew more about me than I did. She had the answers that I needed to hear. I couldn't wait for Doctor Grey. I now felt frustrated that I'd left that meeting with Rene. She could have told me everything yet I chose not to hear it. I was a coward. I stopped Chloe in the hall on the way to her room and explained my situation.

"Not out here." She said and bustled me into her bedroom. "So you wanna know do you? Well I can only tell you what I know."

I wasn't sure. Do I want to know?

"You've got to be sure you want me to tell you. I really like being your friend and I don't want to loose you over this."

I looked up at her kind face. It's amazing how one changes when you know a person. How their appearance looks completely different. I didn't notice her warts anymore. They had become a part of her and I loved her. I lent forward and touched her hand. "You will never loose me as a friend." I held her gaze. "Ever, I promise."

She stroked my fingers with her hand. "So do you want to know what I know?"

I slowly, closed my eyes and bit my two lips together. I felt nervous. I breathed in deeply. "Tell me what you know."

"How old do you think I am?"

I was puzzled by the question and the change of subject.. "Um, sixteen?" I replied now not so sure.

"I'm twenty five. I came to this hospital when I was fourteen years old."

I looked at her in amazement, "How do you stay so young looking?"

"Well how do you?"

I paused for a moment, not quite knowing what to say. "Well I am still young for starters."

She smiled at me sympathetically. "God I'm gonna get told off by Doctor Grey for doing this. Ok, I saw this in a movie once. Look into this whilst I'm talking to you." She handed me her hand mirror. "Don't look at me, just look at yourself in the mirror."

Without questioning I did as I was told. I hadn't done my make up that day and cringed at the sight of myself.

"I came into this hospital fourteen years ago and I was placed on the psychiatric unit down stairs. I needed help and that was the best place for me. Whilst I was there, every now and then I and the other patience would hear this screaming. I mean real in pain screams. At first the nurses wouldn't talk about the patient, who was in that room. They'd say it was none of our business and to worry about our own lives. For years, this went on. Some days there were screams and shouting. But other days, total silence. I would ask the nurse if the patient was ok. They would assure me they were still alive, but that was it."

I was still looking at myself in the mirror.

"Then one night, it was dead quiet. You could have heard a pin drop. I looked out of my bedroom door. There were no nurses around. That was my chance. I crept along the corridor to the door where the screams were coming from. A light was on. I slowly opened the door and…" She stopped for a moment and slid across the bed. She put her arm over my shoulder and carried on talking. "You were in that room Hilary."

My body froze and I'm sure my heart did too, but I didn't ask her to stop, I didn't want her to stop.

"The walls were padded but you still had some bruises on your legs and arms, I assume the marks were there from them having to restrain you. I will never forget that sight. You were sat on the bed writing, at the time I didn't know what. I walked in slowly so as not to disturb you but the door creaked slightly and you looked up at me."

Her voice started to break and I could tell she was fighting back tears. "You looked so malnourished. Your eyes were dark, your lips chapped. The look you gave me. The look of sheer hatred on your face will stay with me till I die. You put your writing to one side and started to get up. I felt almost Alien to you. You looked like you had never seen anything like me before. Before you got off your bed Doctor Grey interrupted us. He wasn't cross with me for entering. He told me you had been here since 1986 that you had been through an incredible amount and that mentally you were taking time out. I asked for your name, but he said he didn't know it. Oh but Hillary." She paused and kissed the top of my head. "Hillary, I could tell he already was in love with you. The way he sat with you and cradled you, whilst he talked. You snuggled into his chest like there was no where else on earth you would rather be. You were like a child and he your guardian angel. I thought then how lucky you were. Even though you were at the time unbalanced, you had something non of us would probably ever know, you had true love."

Tears were streaming down my cheeks. I was still looking in the mirror and drops of tears splashed gently on the glass.

"But I was *born* in 1986!" I said between sobs. I had my head rested against Chloe and I could feel her Breast shake as she wept with me.

"No you weren't you were born in 1967. You're not twenty Hilary, you're thirty eight."

Before my eyes, I saw myself change from a nineteen year old, to a nearly forty year old. I could see faint signs of wrinkles, that I had never noticed before. My skin looked paler and my mouth thinner.

I didn't think, I was like any of the girls in here, but I was just the same.

"I was in the room for nineteen years. I wonder what happened to me, why was I there, do you know?"

Chloe shook her head. "You'll have to ask Doctor Grey that on."

Nurse Sarah came in. We must have fallen asleep, it was dark outside. I had a crick in my neck because of the way I had been lying.

"I think you should be in your room now. It's time for lights out."

I nodded sleepily. I stood up and Sarah put her arm around me. I looked back at sleeping Chloe. She looked so peaceful and carefree. I thought about the things she had related to me. The information that she had bestowed upon me was going to change my life forever. Oddly enough, as I climbed into my own bed and snuggled down, I felt excited. I was beginning to know who I was. I knew it was going to be thrilling and terrifying. But I knew I wasn't going it alone. I had Chloe and Doctor Grey to hold my hand every step of the way.

My room was dark and my eyes followed the shadows and the

patterns of light over the walls and across the ceiling. Then my eyes rested on the picture of my mother. She had looked different in the picture Rene had shown me. I flicked on my lamp and clambered across my bed. I lifted the picture down off my shelf and studied it. I looked at the way she was smiling, the way her eyes creased at the corners. I looked at her hairline and the shape of her nose. I crawled over to my mirror and held the picture out in front of me then studied my own face. No wonder she did not look like my mum. The lady in the picture was me.

Chapter Twenty one

Christmas day had finally arrived. Luckily Justin was visiting their Aunt so James and I had the whole Christmas weekend to ourselves. We had breakfast in bed together and we opened our stockings by the open fire in his bedroom. Penny and Polo had their own stockings too. They both had pet sweets and chews and were occupied with them all morning.

James had a surprise for me. He had opened up the old hall where his parents used to have dinner parties. It was huge. The long table in the center of the Hall could seat twenty-eight people but we sat ourselves in the nearest corner to the kitchen.

The dinner was beautiful we had roast turkey and roast duck, roast *and* mashed potatoes with steamed vegetables.

We talked about past Christmas' with our families and laughed at how chaotic they were. James has twelve cousins and six nieces and nephews and they all usually had Christmas here as James has the biggest house. We giggled over the thought of his big family crammed into one little house.

Then I thought of Jennifer. I hoped she was ok. When she found out she was pregnant with me she had run away from home and has never seen her family since. I hoped she wasn't alone for Christmas.

"I hope Jennifer is ok." I said to James during our Christmas pudding.

"You want to go and see her this afternoon?" He asked and pushed a strand of my hair back from my face.

I wanted to see her but I was still so angry with her and myself for getting into this mess that I didn't want to ruin what a happy day James and I were having. Jennifer and I were bound to argue.

"No, I tried to talk to her again yesterday, but Marie said she wasn't there. Anyway she'll probably be with Jim's family. She may not even be home."

James nodded in response. "Fair enough. But if you change your mind." He kissed me then put some more cream onto my pudding. After we had washed up our dinner things we snuggled up together in the cozy little front room and opened our main presents. James had been given a lot of presents. He got mostly clothes, like ties, socks and shirts for work. He got a new suit jacket from his Aunt and a pair of jeans from Justin. I got a lovely silver necklace from Lillian, of which I felt bad about, because I had not given her anything.

There was one present left for each of us to open. Polo had been my Christmas present from James and he had also spent a fortune on my dress and shoes so I had told him not to get me anything else. He had also made me agree not to get him anything because of my financial situation.

"Now, I know you told me not to get you anything, but I couldn't not. So here." And I handed him his last little present that was left under the tree.

He shook his head in disagreement but took it anyway. He riped the wrapping paper off and inside was reveled a blue box and in there were two pearl cuff links I had had engraved.

"From Mia." He read the first one. "With love." The second. "They are beautiful Mia, thank you so much." He lent forward and kissed me tenderly on the lips.

I looked around the tree, the presents had all been opened but one. My one from Jennifer.

I sat and stared at it for a while. The wrapping paper had been thrown on. It looked like a hurried job. Old feelings of bitterness came back. Bet she quickly wrapped it to give it to me that night to make me feel guilty.

James caught my attention. He tilted his head and lovingly said. "It won't unwrap its self."

I smiled weakly, lent over and pick it up. It was heavier than I had expected and tumbled forward slightly.

"Whoops." James giggled giving me a helping hand.

"I wonder what it could be." I said holding it in my hands. I felt like I wanted to savour the moment. Just hold it before opening it. I had not asked for anything so had no idea what it could have been.

"Well you won't know unless you open it…What's the matter Mia?" James asked concerned.

"I don't know." And I didn't know. I just felt suddenly humble and in no rush.

Finally my curiosity got the better of me and I riped off the wrapping paper. In shock and surprise I placed the gift gently in my lap. It was Jennifer's Journal. She had kept it from the day I was born. Her thoughts and the stories of her day went into it. She had also cataloged all my milestones in there. No one, not even I was ever aloud to read it.

"Jennifer's Journal." I looked at James. He looked slightly puzzled but looked pleased because I seemed to be happy.

I opened the hard front cover and a letter slipped out. The paper was yellow with age and the writing had faded in the crease of the folds. I read it out loud to James. It was hard to read but I did my best.

"To my darling baby Mia, you had a rather strange birth and I apologies for that. I did my best to get to a hospital but my work at

the time did not permit me. But I promise from now on I will do my utmost to keep you safe, happy and forever loved. I will never leave you. I am always with you even if you cannot see me. I love you my little Mia. My precious little girl. " Written at the bottom of the page it read, in new writing. *Turn to the page marked with thread.*

I lifted the book up to look at it from the side. There was little peace of cotton marking the middle of the book. I ran my finger along it and opened the page. It was such a big book that it took up my entire lap.

A twisting feeling gripped my chest as I read what was written in Jennifer's handwriting at the top of the page. *You may start where I have now left off.*

"Something is wrong!" I gasped. I placed the journal on the floor and jumped to my feet. "We have to go and see Jennifer!"

James nodded. He didn't ask any questions he just grabbed his coat and boots and headed for the door.

"Why would she give me her journal!" It was a rhetorical question. I had a sense of dread in my stomach and my chest ached.

We stepped outside into the cold night. The frosty wind took our breath away.

"What's that smell?" James looked at me and we both sniffed the air.

"Smoke!" I said "Oh my god Jennifer!"

"No." James said doubtfully but saw me starting to run so ran after me.

We took the back alley that ran behind James' house. There was smoke coming from the apartment. Billows of smoke rose and blackened the sky. I ran faster, I could feel my heart racing in my chest. As we got closer I could see hoards of people standing in the streets talking excitedly. I pushed my way through the crowds to the fireman at the front. There were at least twenty men still trying to put out the blaze.

"Jennifer!" I called out and eagerly looked around. "Jennifer!"

"Excuse me miss." Said one of the Firemen taking my arm.

"My mother, Jennifer Preston. Where is she, is she ok?" I was still looking around anxiously.

The Fireman looked at me then looked over at the burning building. That was it. That was all he needed to do.

"No!" I screamed and started running towards the burning apartment. I felt the Fireman and James grab both my arms and pull me back.

"Let me go!" I screamed but James kept a firm grip. I tried to heave myself away from him again. I had to get to her, but James held on to me tightly. He pulled me down to my knees and held my arms whilst I struggled to get free.

"Mia, Mia." He repeated softly, his voice shaking with emotion. "Mia."

I stopped fighting and clung to him, crying deeply.

"My Mummy's in there." I cried. "I want my mum."

Chapter twenty two

I could still smell the burning in my nostrils as I sat up shaking in my bed. I had had the nightmare of my mother's death again and I always wake up feeling the same. Frightened and alone. I clambered out from the muddle I had made of my bed sheets and wrapped my dressing gown around me. I opened my bedroom door a little. The hallway was dark and the nurse was not at her station. I crept down the corridor to the double doors at the end. No one seemed to be about so I made my way down the stairs. I don't know what made me do it but I headed for the psychiatric ward.

The ward looked the same as mine apart from the doors. The doors down there looked a lot heavier and where we had windows in our doors they just had bars.

My hair prickled up on my neck. I don't know why I was down there but something has drawing me in. I walked slowly down the cold stone hall. Doors were placed evenly either side of me and I felt very enclosed. Then a feeling came over me to turn to my right and face a certain door. My heart pounded within my chest and my palms started to sweat. I lifted my hand slowly and pressed down on the door handle. The door stuck and I had to push on it hard to open it. I pushed so hard that when the door opened I fell forward into the room.

I straightened myself up and looked around. All the walls were padded with big gray cushions hung from the ceiling. There was one window that let the moon light shine in. It lit the bed up at the far end of the room with a blue light.

Then it started happening again, sitting in front of me on the bed was me. I looked straight into her eyes. She looked dead. Her eyes were sunken and her hair had been shaved. Her lips were dry and had no colour to them.

Chloe was right I had such hatred in my eyes. I tried to look away but I was frozen to the spot. Then without wanting to I slowly walked towards the bed. Chains were still laid out upon it and I moved one so I could sit down next to my ghost. She turned and looked into my eyes. My heart stopped beating. I wanted to scream out but I couldn't. I was trapped, in this moment, with her.

"What happened?" I finally managed to ask.

I then heard a lot of bustling and moving about, people all talking together. I could smell beer and sweat and hear music playing. I looked around, I was no longer in the cell I was in the brothel again. "What ever happens I won't run away." I told myself. I felt the urge to go outside. I dodged and weaved in and out of the cackling prostitutes and found the exit. I stepped out into the street. The ground was covered in snow. To the right of me a couple were kissing against the wall and to my left was the back entrance to Hyde Park. I looked down the street and I could see some men busy taking down Christmas decorations.

I've lived here, I thought to myself. I stepped out and looked up at the big towering building. This was once my home. I then looked down at myself, I had changed. I was wearing heels a short skirt and a top that didn't quite cover my navel. I then saw myself taking a man by the hand and leading him inside. I followed them into a small room with a bed. The man was well dressed, he was wearing a suit with a tie and had pearl cuff links on his shirtsleeve. He kissed the other me lovingly and stroked her cheek.

"I've missed you." He said softly and I watched him kiss me again. He was affectionate, not at all like the other man I had seen in my visions before. I watched him lay me down on the bed and slowly and gently make love to me. When he had finished he left his money on the nightstand and left.

I suddenly felt an over whelming sensation in my stomach I gripped my arms around my middle and doubled up in pain. It felt like excruciating cramps. I then felt water gush out from inside of me and trickle down my legs. I managed to stand upright to see that I wasn't in the brothel anymore, I was in some toilets. I had the gripping pain again. The man that seemed to be with me said that he would go and get help. He zipped up his trousers, tucked in his shirt then ran out the door leaving me in a heap on the floor. I lent my back against the bathroom wall still gripping my stomach I noticed that it was a lot bigger.

"What's going on?" I screamed. I was scared but that was soon over ridden by another incredible cramping pain. I had had this pain before I thought, a very long time ago. I was in labor. A paramedic came rushing into the bathroom.

"Come, we've got to get you out of here."

"No." I heard myself saying. "Please don't move me."

"It's to late, we'll have to do it here, she's coming." He said to his colleague.

The rest of what happened was a blur. I was pushing, but what was said or done I don't know.

Then the paramedic called we're losing her and I thought to myself, I'm not going anywhere. I finally managed to focus and realized he was not talking about me. Over in the corner I could see them trying to resuscitate a tiny little baby. My baby, she looked no bigger than my hand. I tried to move but another paramedic held me down.

"You must stay." She said.

"No." I screamed. "I want my baby!" I looked over at them in the corner. One looked up at the lady holding me and sorrowfully shook his head.

"No!" I wailed. "No, No, No!"

"We've lost her. Better get them both to the hospital."

My world crashed around me. Everything stopped.

I was awoken from my trance by the lady paramedic.

"Excuse me, excuse me miss?"

I looked up at her.

"What was your babies name so we can write it on her tag?"

"Mia." I said softly. "My babies name *is* Mia."

* * *

I woke up on the bed startled. My body felt clammy and hot. My head was pounding and I still had a slight aching in my groin. I sat up on the bed and tried to adjust my mind, as to where I was. I then saw myself, sickly and thin, standing at the foot of the bed.

"You're free now," she said, "Now you know, who you were and what you went through, so find out who you are now. Go to him, Go to him." She repeated and with that she disappeared.

I sat on the bed and tried to peace together what I had just experienced. I was a prostitute, I seemed to have had a love of what looked like quite a rich man and I had a baby who was still born named Mia. "Mia!" I said out loud. "Oh my god!" I ran out of the ward and down to A & E. I didn't bother to look around for anyone I just ran straight to Doctor Grey's apartment.

I banged on the door hard with my fist and eventually I saw a light come on. Doctor Grey's sleepy head peeped out between the frame and the door.

"Hilary?" He cleared is throat. "Everything ok?"

"Not quite, let me in."

He closed the door and I heard him take off the chain. He yawned as he opened it again for me.

"Put the kettle on." I demanded and sat down on the seat where I had sat the last time I was there.

I was itching with nerves and excitement. I couldn't keep my legs still. It was also quite cold in the room, which didn't help.

"Here." He handed me my coffee and then sat opposite me on the other armchair. He took a sip of his tea then looked up at me. "Ok, what has happened?"

"I'd get your pad out." I said.

He pointed to the coffee table that was next to me. There was my journal in its new folder I had been given for my birthday and on top of that was his notebook. I handed him his notebook and I kept my journal.

"You read it all?" I asked him.

He nodded and clicked his pen.

I explained to him what had happened in the psychiatric unit, what I had seen in my vision.

"I'd had a baby." I said. I started to feel a lump rise up in my throat. "So that's why I'm in here, when my mother died I must have run away and started working on the streets."

Doctor Grey stared down at his notebook and nodded his head. "Look in that draw under the coffee table. There are two pieces of paper in there. Get them both out."

I leaned over and fished the two pieces of paper out of the draw. They were two birth certificates. I read them out loud.

"Jennifer Preston, born May first, 1967." Then the other. "Mia Preston, born June first 1986." I looked up at Doctor Grey. "But, I don't understand."

"It is true that your mother died in a fire. She died in 1980 along with your father. *Her* name was Hilary Preston. You couldn't cope with the loss of your mother, so you ran away. Your sister Rene tried to find you but to no prevail. It seemed you just disappeared off the face of the earth.

In memory of your mother, you must have changed your name and now we know what you were doing. You fell pregnant and had the baby too soon and she died. That sent you a little too far over the edge and that's how you ended up in here."

I shook my head, I couldn't quite take it all in. "No, I changed my name when I came in here to protect myself. I named my baby after me, I'm Mia Preston." I held up the birth certificate with my name on it.

"No, you are Jennifer Preston. This." He said pointing to my journal, "This is all a lie. You couldn't cope that Mia died, so, whilst you were in here you made this whole life up for her. This never happened Jennifer. It never happened, it's just a story."

"My name is Hilary." I said feeling angry.

"No, your name is Jennifer, you are Mia's mother." He tapped my journal with his index finger and added softly "You made Mia live on through you."

I looked down at the floor. It all made sense. What Chloe had said, my dreams and now what Doctor Grey was telling me.

"Where, where did you get this?" I asked, my voice breaking as I held up the birth certificates.

"I made some calls to the hospital. When we went for our ice cream the first time and you recognized the place I knew you had been there before, so I knew which part of London you were from. Then, when you gave me your journal, I had some names I could find. Of course, asked for Hilary Preston first, but your ages didn't match up. But then that led me to Rene. I then tried Mia Preston and they sent me a copy of her birth and death certificates. The dates matched and it made sense. I got your birth certificate from Rene."

I wiped a tear away from my eye. I felt that sense of despair I had when my mother died and then when Mia died, I felt like I had lost them both all over again.

"So, I'm not Mia. All that is written in my journal, I wrote when I was in here, I never lived it?" I paused to take it all in. "So I never did any of that stuff. I never lived in all those different countries. I didn't travel around with Jennifer being her run around, but it all seemed so real." I looked down at my journal, at my life that I had never even lived. It just seemed so real. "I'm Jennifer and Mia, who I thought I was, died before she even lived." I started to weep. Everything I knew, everyone I knew, disappeared before my eyes. "What, what about James?" I said through sobs.

Doctor Grey sat down at my feet and rubbed my knees. "That man you saw at Hyde Park, you remember, that day we went for ice-cream?"

I nodded. I knew where he was going with this. "He was the man from my vision. He used to be one of my clients." I cried even more.

"Are you ok?" He asked cautiously.

I shrugged. "It's all just swings and roundabouts in the end, isn't it."

Doctor Grey didn't say anything else, he sat with me and held me.

* * *

A few days later I had another visit from Rene and she filled in the gaps. She came six times after that, so we could start to build a new relationship with each other. I started to remember her quickly. I remembered playing with her when we were little, we didn't to get along, to begin with, but as we grew older, we became really close. She reminded me of Jennifer, well me. She had slight air of pride about her, we held ourselves in the same way. She told me how I used to go to acting class and was dying to be an actress, on the stage. Our parents used to travel a lot with work and would leave us in the care of our nanny, Lillian. She had also told me how our parents had left me a vast sum of money, when they had died. It had been sitting in an account for so long that it had doubled, nearly tripled in value.

The school that I saw, when we were in London, used to be the apartment where I had lived as a Street walker. Doctor Grey explained to me that it was me who had burnt down the apartment building. I had managed to get everyone out and set it alight. He said it was from the trauma of loosing my baby. The firemen had managed to get me out, but I had run away before they could see to me. I had booked myself into the hospital. I gave them my mothers name and that was it, that was the last time I had spoken until a few months ago.

I had a session with Doctor Grey every other day, for four weeks to help me piece together my past and get me ready to go back out into the world. A lot of memories came back through those sessions, but I still had no memory of being in the psychiatric word. My Journal seemed to me, to be the only truth, the only thing I could remember, that fills in those years, lost. But, I had to stop lying now, I could see that. I had to learn to except my past, so I could progress in building my future.

They held a party for me on my last day. There were tears of joy and sadness. Chloe and I promised to stay in touch and as soon as she got out we would go on holiday together.

Doctor Grey met me at the entrance of the hospital and we walked down the steps together.

"So what now?" He looked at me. He had a sad look in his eyes.

"I've just got to wait for Rene to come and pick me up. She said she'd be here for three."

He looked at his watch, then looked down the road. "I mean us, Jennifer?"

I looked at him, his eyes were red and his body was stiff.

I was getting used to people calling me Jennifer. I was beginning to like it.

"I know it's really unprofessional and I know you've just been through an awful lot, but you see." He stepped forward and took both my hands in his. "I'm in love with you. Even when you were in that room and you never spoke, all you did was your writing." He paused and smiled at me. "Oh but the way you were with me. The way you seemed to light up, when I came into the room. Jennifer I swear you loved me too."

"You were James."

"Pardon me?"

"This man I concocted in my mind was modeled on the man who used to pay me for sex. But his soul, his kindness and never giving up on me, was modeled on you. Yes Robert I did love you, and I still do. I am so in love with you."

He pulled me forward and kissed me hard on the lips. A tear escaped my eye and rolled down my cheek onto his lip. He gently pulled away and wiped another tear off my cheek.

"But I need time." I said. "Give me a year. Let me find out who I am first, then we can find out who we are." He nodded slowly, he knew what I was saying was right.

"We can still be friends. We can go for ice creams and to the movies. I don't want to completely cut you out of my life, I just want to take a step back for a while, would that be ok?"

"That would be fine." He kissed my forehead, "Ok then, well here is my private number." He said handing me a piece of paper. "I've got yours so that's ok. Let's arrange to have a picnic next Tuesday. I'll pick you up from Rene's house, at eleven?"

"I would like that." I heard the crunch of stones as Rene's Ford came up the drive.

I threw my small bag in the back and walked round to the passenger seat. I looked back at him, he seemed so tall and strong yet he looked so lost.

"I'm going to miss seeing you everyday."

"Me too." I said softly. The lump had risen in my throat again. "I'll see you on Tuesday Robert."

"I like it that you're calling me Robert now." He smiled. "Yes Jennifer, I will see you on Tuesday."

Epilogue

Three years later Robert and I were married. We live in Robert's cottage in the country. We have twin girls named Mia and Lilly and have a tabby cat called Penny and a Dalmatian called Polo. Robert and I now run our own clinic in the country for, as I call it, Lost Children. I am finally happy in my own life. I no longer need to pretend. I now know if you search long enough and try hard enough, happiness can be for everyone.

The End

A Romance Based Around Socks,

Emma Hydes, exciting and adventurous new love story, is a tale of one women, two loves and the man she's destined to be with.

"You have to go." I whispered softly and kissed his cheek. I stood up and pulled him to his feet. He lent down and kissed me softly on the lips and I felt a tear of his roll down onto my cheek.

"Come with me!" He said with a plea.

"I can't, my life is here."

"Then I'll stay with you, I wont go." He kissed me again, harder this time.

"Noah we've talked about this, you must go, you can't stay because of me, I will not be the one who ruins your life."

"But I love you!" He pulled me into his embrace. "I can't leave you."

My heart ached, I always new this day would come but, you can never prepare yourself for the heart ache when it does. I had lived with this boy in my life for so long that I had forgotten, and was not quite sure how to live without him. But I was not going to ask him to stay. I couldn't do that to him, because I knew he would stay and then regret it for the rest of his life, which, would then lead on to him hating me. I could not live knowing he hated me. "I love you," I said "And our love will stretch over that big wide ocean, you'll see." I sounded stronger than I felt.

"Really? I will write to you every day telling you how much I love you."

I smiled and kissed him. "I will miss you." I pulled away as one of his friends called to him again.

"I don't know why we're getting so upset you'll, be home for Christmas and that's only..." My voice trailed off as I realised that that was over seven months away.

His friend called again.

"I'm coming!" Noah shouted back frustrated. He picked up his rucksack and swung it over his shoulder. I took his outstretched hand in mine and we walked together to the van. "Sorry guys, we were just saying goodbye."

"I know mate but our plane leaves in four hours and we've got to get across London yet. Hi Em." He added and gave me a little wave. "We'll look after him, don't worry."

"Yeah make sure he don't run off with some American bird!" Said another band mate in the back.

"Shut up!" Noah snapped and punched the boys arm. He then turned his attention back to me. "I love you," he whispered holding my hands up to his lips. "Seriously, I love you and I *promise* I will always love you."

"You better keep that promise!" I kissed him and reluctantly let him get into the van. "Let me know how the recording session goes!"

"I will, I'll call you when we land." He blew me a kiss and gave me a wave as the driver sped off down the road.

I stood watching the empty street, waiting. I hoped that maybe he would come back, but he didn't. Tears stung the backs of my eyes but, I blinked them away. I didn't quite know what to do with myself. My best friend Ann had moved to Canada two months ago. There was always Claire and 'Tasha but I wasn't in the mood to see them. Every evening after college I would either go to Noah's or he'd come to mine.

I looked over at the empty collage. It stood tall and dark as the sun slowly crept behind it and a long shadow was cased over the playing field. It stood grand, but alone and in a way I pitted it. It was so full of life earlier, buzzing with noise and now, like myself, it stood alone. I then looked over my other shoulder to the long row of bungalows situated on the other side of the road. A few curtains twitched as a few elderly people watched me standing alone. Some probably sympathetic and maybe understood what had just happened. Some probably keeping a close eye on me to check that

I'm not waiting for a big gang of kids and rob them. Although saying that, considering they live right by the college, they never seem to have any trouble with the pupils.

A few cars passed, then one of them did a wheel spin, pulled up and stopped beside me and Claire popped her head out of the drivers window. "Want a lift hun'?" She asked with a grin.

I looked at the triangular sign on top of the car it read 'Sally's Driving school.' "You're in the middle of a driving lesson!" I exclaimed.

"Nah, that's all right, hop in."

"You can't just pick up friends in the middle of you're lesson," Came a voice from inside the car, "Besides I'm only insured for one."

"Excuse me!" Claire turned to look at her, "I pay you nearly thirty pounds an hour *and* I'm the one in the divers seat so if *I* wanna take my friend home I will."

I raised my eye brows in surprise. I knew my friend was out spoken but not that much. Her parents owned half the pubs in Hawkshead which was near to where I lived, I think Claire thought because of this she could act how ever she liked. I liked her very much, she was very giving and excepting on many things but sometimes I found her just a little too much to take. "I'm all right sweety, you go ahead, I'll probably see you tomorrow."

"Has Noah gone?" She asked, carefully.

"Excuse me miss the clock is ticking." Came the voice of the instructor again.

"Yes but who's paying? God!" She turned back to me and smiled sweetly.

"He has, but I feel I want to be alone for a little while."

"You sure?"

"Yeah, go on enjoy your lesson. I will be fine."

"Ok, if you're sure. Call me later." She revved the engine, blew me a kiss and whizzed off down the road, leaving me in a cloud of smoke.

That poor women. I thought of the instructor clinging on for dear life. I had been in the car with Claire before and it was an experience I will never forget.

I looked down at my feet. I felt very sorry for myself and also very lonely, but if I couldn't be with Noah this evening, then I wanted to be alone. I breathed in deeply and let the air out slowly. "He is gone," I said to myself as if just realizing. "Now it's time for my life to begin." I kicked the few pebbles that lay in front of me and slowly headed for home.

An extract from **A Romance Based Around Socks,** available February 2009....

EMMA HYDES, from a young age started to write stories and would read them to the younger pupils of her school.
She gathers ideas for her books from her own experiences and others lives around her.
She is a young mother who,
currently lives and writes in the Cotswold's.